THE LEGEND TAKES A FALL

As the buggy went over, Clint felt himself tossed ass over teakettle to the ground. He landed hard on his back, the wind rushing from his lungs. He stared up at the sky and was aware of gunshots. He heard a horse whinny and run off, a woman yell, and then a man cry out. Painfully, he rolled himself over and reached for his gun. As he did so, he suddenly felt himself get kicked in the ribs, and then somebody was standing on his gun hand. . . .

"What an unfortunate accident," Louis said.

Clint stared into the barrel of a gun. . . .

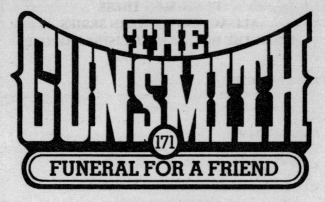

THE GUNSMITH

171

FUNERAL FOR A FRIEND

J. R. ROBERTS

JOVE BOOKS, NEW YORK

FUNERAL FOR A FRIEND

A Jove Book / published by arrangement with
the author

PRINTING HISTORY
Jove edition / March 1996

The Putnam Berkley World Wide Web site address is
http://www.berkley.com

ISBN: 0-515-11829-X

A JOVE BOOK®
Jove Books are published by The Berkley Publishing Group,
200 Madison Avenue, New York, New York 10016.
JOVE and the "J" design are trademarks
belonging to Jove Publications, Inc.

PRINTED IN THE UNITED STATES OF AMERICA

10 9 8 7 6 5 4 3 2 1

ONE

Under ordinary circumstances Clint Adams would have thoroughly enjoyed the prospect of a trip to Chicago, but these circumstances were anything but ordinary.

He was going to attend a funeral—a funeral for a friend.

Word of Jack Miller's death came to Clint in Labyrinth, Texas. Miller was one of those friends you rarely see and never forget. It didn't matter to Clint that he hadn't seen Miller in—what, three or four years? When he heard that the man had died he knew he had to go to Chicago to attend the funeral.

"You ever mention this fella to me?" Rick Hartman asked.

They were sitting at his table in Rick's Place, his saloon.

"I probably have, over the years," Clint said. "It's funny, though."

"What is?"

"That the funeral is in Chicago."

"Well, isn't that where he lived?"

"No," Clint said, "I mean, not that I know of. I don't remember him ever mentioning Chicago to me."

"But you're still going to go?"

"He's still dead," Clint said. And he left for Chicago the next day, leaving Duke, his big black gelding, behind and making most of the trip by rail. What he couldn't do by train he did by coach.

He'd been notified of the death by telegram. That was the other odd thing. The telegram was unsigned. Rick reminded him that he'd walked into a trap once before because of a message, but Clint genuinely thought this was different. Still, when he got off the train in Chicago he was not only wearing his modified Colt in his holster, but the little Colt New Line he favored was tucked into his belt, beneath his shirt.

He'd traveled light, taking only a small carpetbag. It wasn't long ago he'd carried this same bag to Seattle, and hadn't that turned into a mess? What could happen here, though? After all, he was just attending the funeral of a friend, wasn't he?

Clint took a horse-drawn cab from the station to a hotel he had stayed in before called the Michigan House. The name came from the fact that it was located on Michigan Avenue.

"How long will you be staying, sir?" the man asked.

"I'm not sure," Clint answered, signing the register. "At least a couple of days." He was relieved when the clerk behind the desk, a short man with mutton-chop whiskers didn't recognize him. It was always awkward for Clint when strangers recognized him by name or appearance. He preferred it this way.

"Do you need help with your luggage?"

Clint picked up his bag and said, "I only have this."

"How about someone to show you to your room?"

"No," Clint said patiently, "thank you. I'll find my own way, if you'll just give me my key."

"Certainly, sir," the clerk said, handing him a key.

"Thank you."

Clint walked to the stairs and ascended to the second floor. He found his room, entered, dropped his bag on the bed, and walked to the window. Looking out the window was a reflex after all these years. It was not uncommon for him to be followed to hotels. It was afternoon, and there was a lot of activity on Michigan Avenue. If someone had followed him he couldn't see him from here.

He went to the bed and sat down on it. He didn't know where Miller's family lived, only where the funeral parlor was. He knew that because the mysterious telegram he'd gotten had given the address. It was after three, though, and he didn't know if the place would be open for visitation. No, that was an excuse. The truth was he didn't want to encounter any of the family until he had some idea of what had happened.

Abruptly, suddenly struck by an idea, he got up from the bed and strode purposefully from the room. There was a way he could find out what he wanted to know without waiting to talk to the family.

TWO

Clint reached the offices of the *Chicago Tribune* by four P.M. It was on Michigan Avenue, not far from the hotel, so he had been able to walk it. He hoped that he would find someone on duty in the morgue.

He had not been to the *Trib* offices in a long while, but he recalled that the morgue was—fittingly—in the basement. He identified himself to the guard on duty in the lobby and was allowed to pass, but only to go to the basement.

Halfway down the stairs the musty smell of old newspapers hit him. When he got down there he found an elderly gentleman sitting at a desk. He did not recognize the man, although he seemed to remember a man much like him working there the last time he was there.

"What can I do for you?" the man asked.

"I'd like to see your obituaries for the past week."

4

He wasn't sure when Miller had died, or when the obit might have run. In fact, he wasn't even sure he was in time for the funeral.

"There's a fee," the man said.

Clint shrugged and said, "Okay."

"It ain't much," the old man said. "Nothin's for free anymore."

"You said it," Clint said, and paid the nominal fee.

"Sit over there and I'll bring 'em over."

"Thanks."

Clint went to the table the man indicated and sat down. It only took a few moments for the man to return with a small stack of papers.

"Lookin' for anybody in particular?" he asked as he set them down in front of Clint.

"A friend," Clint said.

"Too bad," the man said, and walked away.

Clint started going through the papers and found what he wanted in a five-day-old issue. The obituary was brief:

JACK MILLER was found dead in his home, cause not yet revealed. The matter is under investigation by the police. He is survived by his mother, uncle, two sisters and brother. The funeral will be held up until the body is released by the police, but will be held at . . .

It gave the name and address of the funeral home, which Clint already had.

"I'm done," Clint told the old man on the way out.

"Find what you wanted?"

"Yes and no."

"Like most things," the man said. "When you find

what you been lookin' for, you ain't sure you want it anymore."

"I suppose that's the case."

"You can tell me to mind my own business," the man said, "but maybe I can help."

Clint had an idea that the man just wanted some company, but there was a possibility that he might know something.

"I was looking up the obituary of a friend of mine named Jack Miller."

"Miller," the man said, frowning. "I think I remember that one."

"You do?"

"No cause of death, right? Bein' looked into by the police?"

"That's right. What else do you remember?"

"Well," the man said, making a scratchy sound by rubbing his hand over his grizzled face, "I remember somethin' not bein' right about it."

"How do you know?"

"I listen to what people say," the man said. "Got a reporter here named Tisdale didn't think much of the investigation."

"Is that a fact? Why?"

"I guess you'd have to ask Tisdale."

"Where can I find this Tisdale?"

"Upstairs, I guess, or out on a story."

"Can I get past the guard to go up?" Clint asked

"If you got a good reason," the man said. "Tell 'im you got information about a story. He'll let you up."

"Thanks."

"My name's Smudgy—"

"Smudgy?"

The man showed Clint his fingers, which were covered with dust. He'd leave smudges wherever he went.

"Tell 'im I sent you up. He'll let you pass."

"Thanks again, Smudgy."

Clint took out some money, but Smudgy held up his dirty hands.

"You paid the fee."

"I just wanted to—"

"I just appreciate the company, friend."

"And I appreciate the help."

Clint retraced his steps back to the lobby and told the guard that he had some information for a reporter named Tisdale.

"Is that a fact?" The man was husky, in his thirties, with thick black hair under a uniform cap. A patch on his shoulder said SECURITY.

"Smudgy suggested I go up and talk to him."

"To who?"

"Tisdale."

"Oh," the guard said, looking confused for a minute. "Well, you gotta sign this book if you're goin' upstairs."

"Fine."

Clint signed his name, and the guard allowed him to pass.

"Where would I find him?"

"Who?"

"Tisdale."

The guard looked confused again, annoying Clint, who felt like the butt of a joke he didn't understand.

"Second floor," the guard said, "city room"

"Thanks."

Clint thought he detected a smirk on the face of the guard as he walked away. He found the stairs to the second floor and went up to find out what the joke was.

THREE

On the second floor he found a door marked CITY ROOM and went inside. There were a lot of desks and a lot of people. He stopped the person nearest to him and asked for Mr. Tisdale.

"What?" the man asked, frowning.

"Tisdale," Clint said again, feeling like he was speaking some foreign language first to the guard and now to this man. "Do you have a reporter named Tisdale working here?"

"Uh, sure."

"Well . . . where?"

"First row of desks," the man said, "second desk from the front."

"Thanks."

Clint turned, walked to the first row of desks, then worked his way up to the front of the room until he saw the second desk. There was a woman sitting at it as he approached.

"Excuse me?"

She looked up at him. She had shoulder-length brown hair, big brown eyes, and a small, pretty mouth. Her upper lip was unusual. Clint didn't know what that little indentation under your nose was called, but hers was more pronounced than most. It gave her a very unique look.

"Yes?"

"I'm looking for a reporter named Tisdale," he said.

"Yes."

Clint waited, and when she didn't say anything else he asked, "Is he here?"

"She's here," the woman said. "I'm Tisdale, Julia Tisdale."

Now Clint understood why people had looked at him strangely when he asked for "Mr." Tisdale. Smudgy probably thought it would be funny.

"Is there something wrong?" she asked.

"No," he said, "it's just that no one told me you were a woman."

"Is that a problem?" She looked as if she was about to become insulted.

"No, no, not at all," he said, "except that I feel foolish."

"Don't," she said. "It happens a lot. You're not from Chicago, are you?"

"No, I'm not."

"In fact, you're not from the East."

"Right again."

"Just come in on a train from the West?"

"Yes," he said, "about an hour ago, actually."

"And the first thing you did was come looking for me?"

"Well . . . that's not exactly the way it happened," he said.

"Maybe you should explain the way it *did* happen," she suggested. "And who you are. And what you're here about."

"I will," Clint said, "but can we go someplace else?"

"Like where?"

"I don't know," he said. "Someplace where we can have a drink, and something to eat?"

"Are you asking to buy me dinner?"

"I don't care who buys," he answered, "but I haven't eaten since I got here."

She frowned and he wasn't sure whether she was insulted or not.

"Give me a good reason why I should just pick up and go off with you," she said finally.

"I'd like to talk to you about Jack Miller."

"Am I supposed to know who that is?"

"He's a friend of mine who died recently," Clint said, then added, "or was killed."

"Which is it?"

"I understand you have some doubts about that yourself."

"Who told you that?"

He shrugged and said, "I heard."

"I think there's one of my questions you still haven't answered, mister."

"Oh? Which one is that?"

"Who are you?"

"My name is Clint Adams."

The name obviously meant something to her. She sprang out of her chair, grabbed his arm, and said, "Wasn't I gonna buy you dinner, Mr. Adams?"

FOUR

She took him to a restaurant directly across the street called Horatio's. As they were shown to their table she greeted or was greeted by half a dozen people.

"You're well-known in this town," he said, as they sat down.

"A lot of newspaper people eat here," she said. "Of course, I'm not nearly as well-known as you are."

"Not here."

"Even here in Chicago," she said. "I'm sure if these people knew who I was eating with they'd all be over here asking you for an interview. Instead, they don't know and I get the interview."

"Oh? Is this an interview?"

"Well, you obviously want my help with something, right?"

"That's right."

"And to get my help you've got to be willing to do a favor for me, right?"

He frowned.

"I suppose."

"Well, then we've got an interview, don't we?" she asked.

"That all depends."

"On what?"

"On just how much help you are to me."

"Well," she said, "I can't help until you tell me what you need help with, can I?"

At that moment a waiter interrupted them and they both ordered dinner. She suggested steaks, and Clint took the suggestion since she knew the restaurant. They each also ordered a beer.

When the waiter left she leaned forward and said, "You mentioned Jack Miller was a friend of yours?"

"That's right. I got word that he was dead, but not about how he died. When I got here I checked with your morgue for details."

"That's how you got onto me," she said. "Smudgy sent you."

"I'm not at liberty to say."

She smiled and said, "Protecting your source, just like a newsman."

"Or woman."

"Right."

Their beers came and Clint gratefully drank half of his down. He had trail dust and newspaper dust in his throat, and the cold beer cleared it away nicely. She took a sip of hers and put it down.

"All right, Mr. Adams. What do you want to know?" she asked.

"I want to know what you know about Miller's death."

"Not much," she said, "and that's the problem. Nobody's talking very much about it, not even my regular sources."

"Why do you think that is?"

"I don't know," she said. "If I did, then I'd know more about it, wouldn't I?"

"What's your instinct tell you?"

She looked surprised.

"What is it?"

"You're the first man who ever asked me about my instinct, or even acknowledged that I *had* an instinct."

"You work for a major newspaper," he said. "Somebody must have believed in you."

"Well, if they do they haven't said so."

"I guess it must be hard for a woman, huh?"

"Real rough," she said glumly, but then she brightened and said, "but an interview with you would make it a lot easier."

"First tell me what you feel about Miller's death," he said.

"I think something's very wrong," she said. "I think the police are covering something up, but I don't know what."

"Who can I talk to there?"

"In the police department? I think—wait . . . yes, I think the case was handled by Lieutenant Milsap."

"Milsap. Can you arrange a meeting with him for me?"

"Me? What makes you think I could do that?"

"I thought maybe you knew him."

"No, I just know the name. Milsap's not going to

grant me any meetings. I'm not big enough for that."

"Then I'll have to—"

"But *you* are!" she said, so loud and suddenly that people turned to look at them.

"What did you say?"

She leaned forward and lowered her voice.

"You're big enough to get a meeting," she said. "He'll recognize your name . . . and you could get me in."

Clint sat back and asked, "Would that qualify as a favor?"

She sat back, too, but before she could speak the waiter came with their food. They waited until he had set it all down and walked away.

"Are you saying that if you get me in to see Milsap you won't do the interview?"

"No, I'm not saying that," he said, "but I still haven't agreed to an interview."

"Why don't you want to be interviewed?"

"Because I've been interviewed before, and what I say usually doesn't make it into print."

"Hey," she said, "if you do an interview with me it would be accurate, I guarantee it."

"Well, we'll see about the interview," he said. "Let me hear how you think I could get you and me in to see this Lieutenant Milsap."

FIVE

After dinner they each had another beer and talked a little more.

"Are you going to the funeral parlor tomorrow?" Julia asked.

"I thought I might be too late for that."

"No, tomorrow's the first day. The police held the body for a while. That's another reason why I think there's somethin' goin' on."

"Will you be there?"

"I thought I might stop by," she said. "You never know what will happen at a funeral. Besides, I thought Lieutenant Milsap might be there. Hey, that would be a good time for you to meet him, instead of going to his office."

Clint had liked the idea of going to the lieutenant's office and simply introducing himself, but this might be a more natural way of meeting the man.

"Why don't we go together?" Clint asked.

"How do you think that would look?"

"Why would it look wrong?"

"Well, I am a news reporter, and you're a friend of the deceased—"

"I don't see anything wrong with it," he said, interrupting her. "Besides, I need someone to show me where this place is."

She thought about it a moment, then said, "Okay, then. I'll pick you up in front of your hotel in the morning, about ten."

"Fine."

They argued briefly about the check, but Clint finally relented when she told him that the newspaper would be paying for it.

When they walked outside they stopped right in front of the restaurant.

"What hotel are you in?" she asked.

"The Michigan."

"Oh, that's not far from the office. I'll probably go there first and then pick you up."

"Okay. Are you going back there now?"

"Yes, I still have some work to do. Are you going back to your hotel?"

"Yes," he said. "My trip is starting to catch up with me. I only stopped in my room long enough to drop off my gear."

"You better get some rest, then," she said. "Uh, do you intend to wear that to the funeral?"

"Wear what?"

"That," she repeated, this time pointing at the gun on his hip.

"I usually wear it."

"That might not get you in so good with Lieutenant Milsap," she said.

"If he's going to recognize my name, wouldn't he also expect me to be wearing a gun?"

She thought a moment, then nodded and said, "I guess you're right. I'll see you tomorrow, then. Ten o'clock, in front of the hotel."

"I'll be there."

She stood there for a moment longer until he thought she was going to ask him something else, and then she turned and crossed the street, heading back to her office.

He'd revised his estimate of her age several times since the moment they'd met, but he finally decided she was in her late twenties. Getting a job on the *Chicago Tribune* at that age was, for a woman, quite a feat. While she seemed intelligent and determined, he wondered if there wasn't some other contributing factor he didn't know about.

Yet.

He watched her until she entered her building, then turned left and started walking toward his hotel. Having her walk into the funeral parlor with him might make him feel less awkward. After all, he didn't know any of Miller's family, and he didn't know if Miller had ever told them about him.

He wasn't looking forward to tomorrow.

As Clint Adams walked away from the restaurant he didn't see the man who was watching him from across the street.

He'd also been in such a hurry when he left his hotel that he had not noticed that he'd been followed to the *Tribune* office.

The man had waited outside, watched Clint come out with Julia Tisdale. The man had been prepared to follow them, but they had gone directly across the street to Horatio's. He had remained on the other side of the street, waiting for them to come out.

Now that they had separated he followed Clint back to the hotel, remaining on the opposite side of the street to avoid being seen.

The whole process of following had started at the train station. The man had not known when Clint was coming in, but he'd been watching the train station since the day before. It was necessary, because if he hadn't caught Clint at the station he'd never have guessed what hotel he was at, and he wouldn't have been able to pick him up until the funeral parlor.

And that was someplace he wasn't looking forward to going to.

SIX

Clint rose early the next morning so he could have a bath and breakfast before he met Julia Tisdale in front of the hotel. Upon rising he walked to the window and looked out. Last night when he had returned to his room he'd done the same thing. It had been getting dark, but he'd thought that he'd seen someone across the street watching the hotel. He couldn't be sure, though, and he didn't see anyone now that it was daylight.

When he came out the front door at five minutes to ten Julia wasn't there yet. He took the time to look up and down the street, as well as directly across from him, but didn't see anyone. There were people on the street, of course, but if he was being watched or followed it was by someone who was damned good at it. Of course, he'd been a bit preoccupied yesterday when he'd gone to the *Tribune* office and hadn't noticed anything then. He determined to be extra vigilant at the funeral parlor.

He turned his head to the left and saw a horse and buggy coming. As it pulled up in front of him he saw Julia sitting in the back.

"Come on," she said, waving.

"Good morning," he said as he got in beside her.

"Morning. Are you rested?"

"Very."

"Ready to do this?" she asked as the buggy started forward. "I know how hard it is to go to the funeral of a friend."

"I'm ready, I guess." He took a quick look behind them to see if they were being followed.

"Were you very good friends?"

"Although we hadn't seen each other in years I think we were, yes. There was a time when we saved each other's lives a couple of times. That tends to bring you closer."

She laughed shortly and said, "I wouldn't know anything about that. The closest I ever came to being killed was when I was almost run down by a milk cart when I was a kid."

"Well, it's not like you missed anything, believe me," he said.

"You'll have to tell me about it sometime."

"Maybe."

Julia looked very fetching in a dark gray blouse, black skirt, and matching black boots. Over the gray blouse she wore a leather vest.

"You look very nice," he said, "considering you're going to a funeral."

"Thanks. You don't look so bad yourself."

Clint was wearing a black suit he had bought not

long ago, in Seattle. He had not worn it since he left that city, and it seemed to fit not only the occasion, but Chicago, as well.

"I see you're wearing your gun."

He looked behind them again but didn't see anyone.

"I'd feel kind of naked without it," he said.

"Why do you keep looking behind us?" she asked. "Do you think we're being followed?"

"I'm just checking," he said.

"You have to do a lot of that, don't you?"

"Yes."

"I guess that comes with who you are."

"Yes, it does."

She shook her head and said, "I don't think I could live like that."

"It's not usually a choice, Julia."

"You mean you don't like being who you are?"

"I like who I am," Clint said, "I just don't like who other people think I am, or want me to be."

"Then why—"

"Wait a minute," Clint said, cutting her off. "Is this an interview?"

"No," she said, "this is just me being nosy."

"Well, stop being nosy for a while."

"Can I help it if I want to get to know you better?"

"I've had experience with newspaper people before, Julia," he said. "Usually when they say they want to get to know you better it's time to shut up and look out for yourself."

"Well," she said, "I can see that I'm going to have to do something to earn your trust."

"Not if you forget for a while that you are a newspaperwoman."

"I can't do that, Clint," she said, shaking her head. "I've worked too damned hard to get to where I am, and I want to go further."

"And you think an interview with me will help you do that?"

"Definitely. Face it, like it or not, you're a legend of the West. People love to read about people like you and Wild Bill Hickok and Bat Masterson."

"Hickok and Masterson are worth writing and reading about," Clint said. "They're interesting men who have led interesting lives."

"And you aren't interesting?" she asked. "I think you're just too modest."

"Or private."

"It's sounds funny for a man like you to claim to be private."

"Maybe it's just that I'd like to be private."

"Then why don't you try it? Why don't you try going somewhere and starting over?"

"I have tried, Julia," he said. "It just doesn't work for me. Somebody always recognizes me, or somebody always needs help. *Something* always happens."

"Like a friend dying under suspicious circumstances?"

"Yes," he said, "exactly like that."

SEVEN

When they reached the funeral home Clint stepped down and helped Julia down, then took care of paying the driver.

"You didn't have to do that," she said.

"You bought dinner last night."

There was not much activity in front of the funeral parlor. Clint wondered if everyone was already inside, or if they had yet to arrive.

"Shall we go in?" Julia asked.

Clint paused to look around. If they weren't followed from the hotel, maybe there was someone here watching them. After all, someone had sent him that anonymous telegram.

"All right."

Together they entered the funeral home and were greeted by a man in a dark suit, with slicked-down black hair and a bereaved expression.

"May I help direct you?" he asked.

"Yes," Julia said, "we're here to pay our respects to the Miller family."

"Ah, yes," the man said, shaking his head, "tragic. You will find Mr. Miller in room number five."

"Room five?" Clint asked as they continued on.

"Haven't you ever been to a big city funeral home before?" she asked. "With all your traveling?"

"As a matter of fact, I haven't," he said, surprising himself.

"Well, they have more than one deceased person here, Clint. There are other families saying good-bye to their loved ones."

"You mean the place is full of dead people?"

"Well," she said, "hopefully most of the people in the building are alive, but the guests of honor are all dead."

Most of the visiting he'd done to pay respects had been to small town undertakers, where they usually had one person at a time.

They found room five and stopped just outside. Inside it was darker, but he could see chairs set up. He stuck his head in and saw an open coffin in front of the room. Only the first row of seats was occupied, and he counted five people, three women and two men.

"Not that many people in there," he said.

"Probably just the family. Did your friend have lots of other friends?"

"I don't know."

"Well," she said, "maybe we should go in."

"Miss Tisdale, isn't it?" a man's voice said, before they could move.

They both turned to face the man who was approaching. He looked to be in his early forties, dressed in a charcoal-gray suit and carrying a black hat in his hand. He was tall, broad-shouldered, and carried himself with an easy confidence.

"Lieutenant Milsap," she said. "I'm surprised you know who I am."

"I know all the reporters in town, Miss Tisdale," the lieutenant said, "especially the pretty ones."

"I'm flattered that you remember."

Milsap turned his attention to Clint.

"Are you also a reporter with the *Tribune*?" he asked.

"No," Clint said, "I'm a friend of the deceased."

"Lieutenant, this is Clint Adams," Julia said, hurriedly making the introduction. "He got into Chicago yesterday."

"Oh? From where?" the lieutenant asked.

"I started from Texas."

"And you came all this way to pay your respects, Mr. Adams? You and Mr. Miller must have been good friends."

"We were."

"Where did you know him from?"

"We met in Denver, a long time ago."

"And when was the last time you saw him?"

"I suppose it must be three or four years—probably . . . let me think . . . yes, three years."

"That's a long time for friends not to see each other," Milsap observed.

"Not when you both travel."

"Oh, so Mr. Miller traveled?"

"He did when I knew him."

"Doing what?"

Clint shrugged.

"Traveling."

"And what do you do, Mr. Adams?"

"I travel, also."

Julia looked disappointed at the prospect of Milsap not recognizing Clint's name.

"Lieutenant, surely you know who Clint Adams is?"

"Julia—" Clint said.

"I apologize, Mr. Adams," Milsap said. "I do, indeed, know you by reputation. I guess I was just indulging my curious nature. I just wanted to see how you would describe yourself."

"I see."

Milsap waited a few moments, then asked, "How would you describe yourself?"

"Right now I'm sad about my friend's death and a little nervous about going in to see him this way."

"Ah, yes, I'm sorry," Milsap said. "It must be hard. Please, why don't you go on in. We can talk later."

Clint wanted to ask, "About what?" but decided not to.

"Yes, why don't you go in, Clint?" Julia asked. "I'll entertain the lieutenant."

"Actually," Milsap said, "I was going in myself."

"Good," she said, sliding her arm inside of his, "I'll go with you. I really didn't relish going in alone, and Clint is going to talk to the family."

"And you are not?"

"I don't know them," she said, "and I didn't know the deceased. I'd just be a bother to them."

"You are a rare newspaper person, Miss Tisdale," the lieutenant said, "if you're worried about bothering people."

"Yes, I am, Lieutenant," she said, "I am rare, indeed."

Clint went in ahead of Julia and the lieutenant, and slowly approached the front of the room. The casket was opened and looked to be lined with velvet. He couldn't imagine ever being buried in something like that. A pine box would be good enough for him when the time came.

He wondered if he should stop to introduce himself to the family, but decided to first pay his respects to his friend.

He walked up to the front of the room and was aware that the people in the front row had noticed him and were watching him curiously. He could just barely see the deceased now, dressed in a dark suit, very pale from the undertaker's ministrations. It was funny, he thought, how different people looked when they were dead. The body in the casket did not even look like his friend Jack Miller.

Finally he reached the casket, stared down at the face of his dead friend and frowned. Not only didn't it look like Miller, it didn't look like anyone he'd ever seen before.

The man in the casket was not Jack Miller!

EIGHT

Stunned, Clint continued to look down at the dead man. There was no way he could even have been mistaken for Jack Miller—at least, not the Jack Miller that he had known.

Could this be another Jack Miller? Was the telegram he'd received just an elaborate joke? Or perhaps even a trap?

Clint decided not to turn around just yet. He didn't want anyone to see how stunned he was. He wanted to think this through for a bit.

Obviously, this man's name *was* Jack Miller. There had been an obituary, a police investigation, and the man who had greeted them at the front door—the undertaker?—had said his name. This man's name was Jack Miller; he just wasn't the same Jack Miller that Clint had known—or knew.

Now the question was, was he supposed to be?

"Excuse me."

It was a woman's voice. He turned and found himself facing a very attractive woman in her early forties. She had pale skin and blond hair that was accentuated by the black clothing she was wearing.

"Yes?"

"Did you know my brother?"

Clint stared at her, for a moment at a loss as to how to answer the question.

"I'm sorry?"

"I'm Elaine Miller," she said. "Did you know Jack?"

"Jack? Jack . . . Miller."

"Yes," she said, frowning at him. "Are you all right? You don't look . . . would you like to sit down?"

"Yes," Clint said, stalling, "yes, maybe I better."

She took his arm and walked him to a seat in the third row. The rest of the family turned and watched them.

"You must have been very good friends with my brother for his death to affect you this way."

"Jack . . . and I knew each other in, uh, Denver, among other places."

"Oh, then you knew Jack from out west?"

"Yes, that's right," he said. "Out west."

"We weren't really in touch with him during that period of his life," she said. "He'd had a falling-out with our father and had gone out west to . . . I don't know, I suppose to find himself."

That was in keeping with what Jack Miller had told him when they met. He hadn't mentioned Chicago, but he had said something about getting away from his family.

"Maybe you can tell us a little about him back then?" she asked.

"He, uh, never told you?"

"When he came back several years ago," she said, "he said he didn't want to talk about it."

"Was your father alive when he came back?"

"No," she said, shaking her head, "in fact, he came back for Father's funeral. It was held right here in the same place. We were so happy that Jack had come back, and now . . ."

She started to tear up a bit, and he put his hand on hers, which was in her lap. The movement seemed to startle her a bit. She stared at him but did not move her hand.

"What's your name?" she asked.

"Oh, I'm sorry," he said. "My name is Clint Adams."

"Thank you for coming, Mr. Adams."

"Did Jack ever . . . mention me?"

She shook her head.

"I'm afraid he never talked about the years he spent away from us."

"I see."

"Would you come and meet the rest of the family?"

"Of course."

They both stood and Clint decided to play it out and then think more about it when he left. Maybe he'd even talk to Julia about it. He wasn't sure, though, what he should say to the lieutenant just yet.

If anything.

NINE

Clint went with Elaine to meet the other people seated in front.

"Clint Adams, this is my mother, Ellen Miller."

It was easy to see where Elaine got her looks from. Ellen Miller was in her sixties, but she was still a handsome figure of a woman.

"I'm sorry for your loss," he said, his words sounding inadequate to him.

"Thank you."

"This is my younger sister, Evelyn."

If Elaine was attractive and her mother handsome, Evelyn was beautiful. She was in her early thirties and looked stunning in her mourning clothes. When he took her hand she held onto his a moment or two longer than necessary and gave him a long, level stare.

"A pleasure, Mr. Adams."

"I'm sorry," was all he could think to say.

"This is my brother, Earl."

The Miller family seemed to have a thing for names that started with the letter "E." Where, he wondered, did "Jack" come from?

Earl Miller was in his late forties, dark hair going to gray. He resembled his brother—that is, the Jack Miller who was in the coffin.

"And this is my uncle Jed."

Jed Miller was in his sixties, perhaps even seventy, but he had the firm handshake of a man half his age.

"Thanks for comin'," Jed said.

Clint almost said it was his pleasure but stopped himself.

Clint and Elaine became aware of more people walking in the back at that moment.

"Mother, the Simsons are here," she said. "I think I also see that policeman in the back, with a woman I don't know."

"Elaine, would you . . ." her mother said.

"Yes, mother, of course." She looked at Clint and asked, "Would you excuse me?"

"Sure."

She left him there with the family, and it was Evelyn who stood up to talk to him. She was as tall as her sister, more slender and yet more buxom.

"Did you know my brother well?" she asked.

It was a question he wasn't sure he knew the answer to anymore.

"At one time I did, yes."

"He never mentioned you," she said. "You must have known him when he was out west."

Clint found it curious that except for Elaine—and only for a moment—none of these people seemed especially tearful. Ellen, the mother, did seem distraught, but her eyes were dry, not at all red or bloodshot.

"That's right."

"Tell me something—" she started, but Clint cut her off.

"Your sister is coming with some more people," he said. "I'd better move on."

"Will you be coming to the funeral?"

"When is it?"

"Tomorrow," she said.

"Yes, all right."

"And afterward you'll have to come to the house."

"Okay."

"See you later, then."

He smiled at her and moved along just as Elaine arrived with the other people, a couple about Ellen Miller's age.

Clint walked to the back of the room where Julia was sitting with the lieutenant, bending his ear.

"Ah, Mr. Adams," Milsap said, looking pleased at the interruption. "Paid your respects already?"

"Yes, I have."

"Excellent. Will you be staying around?"

"Uh, I don't think so."

"Back tomorrow then? For the funeral?"

"I'll probably be here for the funeral, yes."

"Where are you staying?"

"The Michigan."

"Well, maybe I'll stop by to have a chat."

"Do that, Lieutenant," Clint said. "I'll buy you a drink."

Milsap smiled and said, "I'll take you up on that offer."

"Julia," Clint said, "will you be staying?"

"No," she said, standing up, "I'll leave with you. Thank you for keeping me company, Lieutenant."

"It was my pleasure, Miss Tisdale."

"Let's go," Clint said.

When they got outside Julia said, "What's the hurry?"

Clint had already decided that he had to talk this out with somebody.

"Let's find someplace to have a drink."

"It's too early—"

"Coffee, then."

"I saw you talking to those women," Julia said. "Sisters?"

"Yes."

"Very pretty—"

"I suppose. Someplace for coffee?"

"We can go down here about a block," she said, and they started walking. "What's this all about?"

"I'll tell you when we're sitting."

"Something's wrong, isn't it?"

"There's that keen reporter's instinct."

"What is it?"

"A mix-up," he said, "I hope it's a big mix-up."

The man standing across the street from the funeral parlor watched as Clint Adams and Julia Tisdale walked down the street. He didn't know who the woman was, but she wasn't important. What was important was keeping tabs on Clint Adams without being seen.

He watched them for about half a block and then stepped from his hiding place and followed.

TEN

"Say that again?"

They were sitting at a table with coffee in front of them and he had just told her what the problem was.

"That dead man was not Jack Miller," he repeated. Then he added, "Not the Jack Miller I knew."

She sat back and said slowly, "Yes, he was, Clint. Everybody says so. The papers, the police, the family, they all say he's Jack Miller."

"Well," he insisted again, "he's not the Jack Miller I knew."

"Wait," she said, "you mean there are two Jack Millers?"

"That's one answer."

"What's another answer?"

"Maybe this man isn't Jack Miller."

"Then why is Jack Miller's family crying over him?" she asked.

"There wasn't all that much crying going on that I could see," he said, "but I know what you mean, and I don't know the answer."

"How about another possibility?" she asked, after thinking for a few moments.

"Like what?"

"Like maybe the man you knew never was named Jack Miller."

Clint frowned.

"Just how friendly were the two of you?" she asked. "Did you meet just once?"

"No," he said, "we met in Denver about seven years ago."

"And how many times did you see each other after that?" she asked.

"Oh, over the next four years we ran across each other from time to time."

"How many times is that?"

He thought a moment.

"About half a dozen."

"And each time he was calling himself Jack Miller?" she asked.

"Well . . . no."

"What do you mean, no?"

"Well," Clint said, feeling a bit sheepish. He almost felt as if he was telling tales out of school. "There were a couple of times when he was running from the law, uh, sort of . . ."

Julia frowned as he let it trail off.

"What does 'sort of' mean?"

"Well, Jack—the Jack Miller I knew, that is— wasn't shy about bending the law if he could make a dollar doing it."

"Wait a minute, wait a minute," she said, sitting

forward. "Are you telling me that your Jack Miller was a con man?"

"Um, yeah, I guess that's what I'm saying," Clint said, "a con man and a gambler."

"Well, there it is."

"There what is?"

"If he was a con man, then he conned you, too, into thinking he was Jack Miller."

"Why?"

"For the reason you said, to make money."

"He never made any money off of me," Clint said. "And I already told you, we saved each other's lives."

"But you didn't tell me how."

"I don't know how telling you that will help."

"Can it hurt?"

Clint thought a moment, then said, "Well, I guess not . . ."

"Then tell me."

"Well, the first time it happened was in Denver, after a poker game . . ."

ELEVEN

Denver
Seven years earlier . . .

Jack Miller had been a good enough poker player to be invited to a big game in Denver that Clint, Bat Masterson, and Luke Short had also been invited to. In fact, it was a poker tournament, one of many Clint, Bat, and Short had played in. For Jack Miller, it was the first, and he made it down to the final four with Clint, Bat, and Short. The final winner was Luke Short, who—Clint freely admitted—was the best poker player he ever saw. Bat took exception to that, but Bat Masterson was not a humble man.

Anyway, Clint and Miller had spent a few days together seeing what Denver had to offer after the others had all left. One night they even shared a woman. . . .

·   ·   ·

Clint and Miller were drunk and somehow they had ended up in the company of a woman named Belle Delaney. Belle was an Irish gal who drank right along with them and wouldn't tell them how she got the name Belle, although she agreed that it was not exactly an Irish name.

At one point, when she and Clint were alone, she slipped him her room key and said, "Meet me up there at midnight."

He readily agreed and slid the key into his pocket just before Miller returned. He didn't have the heart to tell his new friend that Belle had apparently picked him over Miller. In fact, the two men had found themselves alone at one point and had discussed who was going to take Belle to bed. They finally decided that she should make the choice.

Finally, Belle announced that she'd had enough and was going to go back to her room. She gave Clint a wink that Miller did not see before she departed.

Clint was wondering how to detach himself from Miller when the other man abruptly announced, "I'm gonna turn in, too."

Relieved, Clint said, "See you in the morning."

As Miller went back to his hotel, Clint went to Belle's and let himself into her room. He was disappointed to find that she was not there, but he felt certain she soon would be. He undressed and got into her bed to wait.

He was there fifteen minutes when he heard a key being fit into the door lock. The door opened and he was shocked to see Jack Miller enter.

"What the hell are you doing here?" he demanded.

"Me?" Miller asked. "What are you doin' here?"

"I was invited," Clint said. He took the key Belle

had given him off the night table and said, "Belle gave me a key."

Miller held up a key and said, "Me, too."

The two men regarded each other for a few moments, and then both started to laugh drunkenly.

"Do you think this is a joke?" Miller asked.

"It seems like something Bat and Luke would dream up," Clint said. "Maybe they hired the woman before they left."

"What do we do now?" Miller asked.

"I think we better get out of here before someone gets the wrong idea," Clint said.

He tossed the sheet aside and stood up. He was standing there naked when another key went into the lock.

"Now who's here?" he wondered out loud.

Miller moved away from the door as it opened and admitted Belle Delaney. She was wearing nothing but a towel wrapped around her, and had obviously just come from a bath. Her red hair was piled on her head, and they could see the freckles that peppered her smooth shoulders and slopes of her breasts.

"Well," she said, "I'm glad you're both here."

"You mean you did invite both of us?" Miller asked.

"Of course," she said, smiling. "You're both so wonderful I couldn't possibly choose. So I thought the three of us could . . . get together."

Clint looked at Miller, while Belle was examining him.

"The three of us?" Clint said. He had never done that before.

"Oh, I don't know . . ." Miller said, shaking his head.

"Well then," she said, "I guess the two of you should choose who stays and who goes."

As if to help them make up their minds she unwrapped the towel from her body and allowed it to drop to the floor. She was magnificently naked. Her skin was flawless, her breasts heavy and firm. The tangle of hair between her legs was a darker red than the hair on her head. Her buttocks were smooth, dimpled and slightly plump, but firm.

Clint felt his penis thickening as he looked at her.

"I think I should stay," he said to Miller, without taking his eyes from Belle.

"Why you?" Miller asked. He was also staring at Belle's body.

"I'm already naked," Clint said.

Abruptly, Miller began to undress, kicking off his boots, dropping his pants and underwear and kicking them away. He tore his shirt off, buttons popping and flying across the room, and in moments he was as naked—and erect—as Clint.

"Oh, my," she said, "you're both lovely."

"You go," Clint said to Miller.

"No, you go," Miller said.

"I have a better idea," Belle said. "I want you both to stay."

She got down on her knees and said, "Come here."

Both men hesitated.

"I said come here!" she said, more forcefully.

Hesitantly they both moved toward her and stopped within her reach.

"Mmm," she said, cradling their testicles in each hand, and then running her hands up and down the length of them. "My, my . . ."

The two men were doing their best not to look at

each other while she caressed them. Clint closed his eyes and suddenly felt her hot mouth swoop down on him. Curiosity made him open his eyes and look. She was sucking on him while stroking Miller with her other hand. Miller was standing there with his eyes closed, a dreamy and somewhat dumb look on his face. Clint wondered if he looked like that when he was with a woman. Suddenly, Belle's head began to bob up and down faster, and he caught his breath and closed his eyes.

This might not be so bad after all. . . .

She switched off, sucking one of them while stroking the other, and when she had both of them painfully full she said, "On the bed."

It soon became obvious that she had done this before. She directed them exactly where she wanted them, and soon Clint was buried inside of her from behind while she sucked on Miller's penis. The men were facing each other, but they soon closed their eyes and surrendered to the pleasure they were giving and receiving. Belle began to moan with her mouth full of Miller. Clint reached for her, rubbing her back, kneading her buttocks, holding her hips so that he could drive into her harder.

Miller held her head and stroked her shoulders while she continued to suck on him. Suddenly his penis was cold. He looked down and saw that she had released him from her mouth and had also removed Clint from her vagina. She reversed her position, and Miller gladly took hold of her hips and drove himself into her from behind.

Clint watched as Belle's mouth took him fully inside and then began to suck him while Miller took her from behind. She moaned loudly and he hoped that Miller would not drive so deeply into her that she might bite him. That would turn pleasure into pain very quickly.

She knew what she was doing, however, and soon Clint found himself spurting into her mouth while Miller roared and emptied himself inside of her vagina.

She extricated herself from both of them and turned over onto her back. She stroked Miller's flaccid penis with one hand and Clint's with the other.

"That was wonderful," she said, "for a start."

Clint and Miller looked at each other for the first time in many minutes, and they were both thinking the same thing.

For a start?

TWELVE

The next morning Clint and Miller both left Belle's hotel with mixed feelings. It had been a wonderful night with her, but both men wondered how glorious it might have been if only one of them had been the object of her attentions.

Glorious for one of them, but not the other.

"Have you ever done anything like that before?" Clint asked.

"No," Miller said. "Have you?"

"No."

"Let's get some breakfast."

"Right."

They started to walk away and Clint said, "I don't think I'd like to do it again."

"Me, neither," Miller said.

They went about a half a block and suddenly Miller shouted, "Look out!"

Clint heard the shot and felt Miller slam into him at the same time. As he fell to the ground he went into a roll and drew his gun. Miller was on the ground, and Clint could see a flash of blood. There was another shot, and he was able to pinpoint it as having come from across the street. When he looked he saw a man in a doorway firing at them. Without hesitation he returned fire as a bullet whined off the wall behind him. He fired twice, hitting the man both times. As the man went down Clint ran to Miller.

"Are you all right?"

"I'm hit," Miller said, "but I'm all right. Check him. Make sure he's dead."

Clint crossed the street, kicked the fallen man's gun away, and leaned over him. He was, indeed, dead.

He went back across the street to see to Miller. . . .

"How badly was he hurt?" Julia asked.

"He'd been shot in the shoulder," Clint said. "He recovered, but if he hadn't pushed me I might have been shot more seriously, possibly killed. He saved my life."

"And you his, by shooting the man."

"No," Clint said, "that didn't count. I saved his life the last time we saw each other."

"Who was the man who shot at you?"

Clint hesitated, then said, "Somebody out to make a name for himself."

Actually, they found out that the man was a suitor of Belle Delaney's. He had followed her to the hotel, saw Clint and Miller, waited for them to come out so he could kill them out of jealousy. Instead, he'd been killed for it.

"So when and where did you save his life?" Julia asked.

"That was three years ago . . ."

THIRTEEN

Dodge City, Kansas
Three years earlier . . .
April 10

This story was a bit more involved, because it also concerned Bat Masterson and his brother, Jim.

James P. Masterson was city marshal of Dodge City when Clint came to town. Bat Masterson, formerly the sheriff of Ford County, in which Dodge City was located, was at that time in Tombstone, Arizona, with the Earp brothers. Wyatt had been a policeman at one time in Dodge City, but he and his brothers had taken their families to Tombstone.

Jim Masterson, as well as being an officer of the law, was also part owner of a saloon in Dodge. It was called the Lady Gay Saloon and Dance Hall, and his partner was A. J. Peacock.

Clint rode into Dodge City on his black gelding, Duke. He was passing through on his way to Texas, and thought he'd stop in and see how Jim Masterson was faring now that brother Bat was no longer in Kansas.

Clint rode up to the marshal's office, dismounted, and entered. Jim Masterson looked up from his desk and smiled at Clint's appearance.

"Clint Adams, you old son of a bitch. How are ya?"

Jim was twenty-six at this time of his life, two years younger than Bat.

"I'm fine, Jim." The two men shook hands warmly. "How are you doing?"

"I'm doin' fine, just fine. How long are you in town for?"

"I don't know," Clint said. "I just rode in. I'm on my way to Texas."

"You in a hurry?"

"Not especially."

"Good, then maybe you'll stay a few days. Hey, come with me over to the Lady Gay and I'll buy you a drink."

"The Lady Gay?"

"Sure," Jim said, grabbing his hat from a wall peg. "I own it now, me and A. J. Peacock."

"You're part owner of the Lady Gay?"

Clint found that odd, since almost exactly three years before Ed Masterson, then marshal, had died as a result of wounds received in a gunfight in the Lady Gay. His wounds had been especially bad, but in spite of it—and in spite of the fact that the muzzle flash had set his clothing on fire—Ed still managed to shoot and kill the two men who'd attacked him. He had then calmly walked across the plaza to another saloon where he announced to his friend, George Hinkle, "George, I'm shot."

He was then taken to Bat's room, where he died with Bat, Jim, and friends around him.

Now Jim owned a piece of that very same saloon. Odd.

"Come on," Jim said, "you look like you could use a beer."

"I could," Clint said. "I've been riding a long time."

They walked to the Lady Gay and entered together. As soon as they walked in, Jim looked unhappy.

"Damn," he swore.

"What is it?"

"That bartender," Jim said. "His name is Updegraff. I talked with Peacock about firing him and he didn't do it."

"I guess you'll have to do it yourself."

"I s'pose," Jim said, "but not today, huh? Today I'm buyin' you a drink."

They walked up to the bar where Jim and the bartender glared at each other for a moment before Jim told him to bring two beers.

"You payin'?" Updegraff asked.

"I don't pay in my own place!" Jim growled. "Get them beers, Updegraff."

Scowling, the man did as he was told.

Clint remembered the Lady Gay from his past visits to Dodge City. It was a saloon and dance hall, and as such it was very big, with a stage at the back. There were also gaming tables strewn about, roulette, faro, and poker, mostly. It was at this point he spotted a familiar face at one of the poker tables.

"Well, I'll be . . ."

"See somebody you know?" Jim asked.

"I do, indeed," Clint said. "That fellow sitting at the second poker table, the one with the black-haired man dealing."

"That's Sam," Jim said. "Damned good dealer. Who's your friend?"

"On the dealer's left," Clint said. "His name's Jack Miller."

"That fella's a friend of yours?"

"That's right," Clint said. "He saved my life four years ago in Denver. He played in a poker tournament with me and Bat."

"I remember," Jim said. "Luke Short won that, didn't he?"

"He did."

"Well . . ." Jim said.

Now it was Clint's turn to ask a question.

"Have you had a problem with him?"

"Not really," Jim said. "I've talked to him."

"About what?"

"Poker, mostly."

"What about it?"

"Well, he keeps winnin'."

"And that's a problem? Oh, wait a minute. You own this place, so he's winning money from you."

"Naw, it ain't that at all," Jim said. "Some of the other players seemed to think he was cheatin'."

"Jack Miller doesn't have to cheat to win, Jim," Clint said. "He's a pretty good poker player."

"Well, now that you told me that, and told me about the tournament in Denver, I can see that."

"He probably didn't like being questioned about his poker playing."

"No, he didn't," Jim said. "We got into it a bit, and

now I feel right bad, since you tell me he's a friend of yours."

"Doesn't look like it affected his playing," Clint said. "He seems to have a small mountain of chips in front of him."

"Well-earned chips, I realize now," Jim said. "I'll have to apologize to him when I get a chance."

"We won't bother him while he's playing," Clint said, "but later on I'll introduce you two."

They finished their beers and Clint said, "I think I'll take Duke over to the livery, and then get myself over to the Dodge House and check in."

"I'll get back to work, but I'll meet you over here later. We'll have dinner together, after you introduce me proper to your friend."

"I'll see you here, then."

Clint left the Lady Gay, retrieved Duke from in front of Jim's office, and headed for the livery.

That's where he was when he heard the shots.

FOURTEEN

Clint dashed out of the livery at the sound of the shots, trying to determine where they were coming from.

"Lady Gay," the liveryman said.

"How can you tell?"

"I been here a long time," the old man said. "I can tell Lady Gay shots from Alhambra shots from Long Branch shots. Thems was from the Lady Gay."

Clint didn't wait to argue with the man. He'd left both Jim Masterson and Jack Miller at the Lady Gay.

When he reached the saloon he rushed in with his gun out, but apparently all of the excitement was over. Jim Masterson was standing at the bar, looking unhappy.

"What happened, Jim?"

Jim looked at him and said, "I guess you could say I fired that son of a bitch bartender."

What had happened was as soon as Clint had left the saloon, A. J. Peacock had come out of the office in the back. He and Jim Masterson had then gotten into an argument over the bartender, Updegraff. Clint didn't know how or why—and neither did Jim Masterson, apparently—but suddenly Updegraff and Peacock had guns out. They fired several shots each at a stunned Marshal Masterson, missing him completely. By the time Jim returned fire they were fleeing and he missed, as well.

"That's a hell of a way to fire somebody," Clint said. "Are you sure you're not hurt?"

"Not a scratch, but I'm pretty pissed I missed them," the lawman said. He ejected the spent shells from his Colt and slid new ones in, then holstered the gun.

"I'm gonna have to find somebody to tend bar," he said. "I'll still see you later back here."

"Wait a minute," Clint said. "Are you going out by yourself?"

"Why not?"

"Jim, they could be waiting out there for you."

"I can take care of myself, Clint."

"Do you have a deputy?"

"No," Jim said. "Nobody will take the job. Do you want it?"

"No," Clint said, "I don't want a badge."

"See?"

"But I'll go with you and watch your back—"

"Clint," Jim said, cutting him off, "believe me, I can take care of myself. Just meet me here later, okay?"

"All right, Jim."

Jim nodded and left.

"Clint? Is that you?"

Clint turned to face Jack Miller.

"Hello, Jack."

"Well, what the hell—" Miller said. "When did you get to town?"

He approached, and the two men shook hands.

"Just a little while ago. Did you see what happened here?"

"Not really. I was concentratin' on my cards and the next thing I know somebody's shootin'. Say, do you know that marshal?"

"I do," Clint said. "He's Bat Masterson's brother."

"Really? I didn't notice a resemblance."

"Have you seen Bat since that tournament in Denver?" Clint asked.

"As a matter of fact, I haven't. It's been a while, hasn't it?"

"About four years, I guess."

"How long since I saw you?" Miller asked.

"Abilene?" Clint asked. "Or El Paso?"

Miller thought a moment, then said, "El Paso, I think it was. A year ago?"

"About that."

"Can I buy you a drink?"

Clint looked at the empty bar.

"Seems they're short a bartender here. Tell you what. Let me get registered in the hotel and I'll meet you back here. I want to introduce you to Jim Masterson properly."

"He tell you we didn't hit it off?"

"He did," Clint said, "but I explained that you don't have to cheat to win at poker."

"Well, that was nice of you to say."

"I didn't say that you won much, though."

"Maybe we'll get a chance to put it to the test while we're here."

"Maybe," Clint said. "It's good to see you, Jack. I'll meet you back here in about an hour. All right?"

"Suits me."

Clint left the Lady Gay and went back to the livery to finish up with Duke, and then to the hotel to finally get registered.

FIFTEEN

Clint took his gear to his hotel room and changed his clothes. He walked to his window and looked down at Main Street. It was getting dark, and from his window he could see the telegraph office across the street. It looked open, and he was struck by an idea.

He hurried from his room across the street. As Clint reached the office the clerk stepped out and began to close the door.

"Hold it, hold it!" Clint called.

The man turned and looked at him.

"I'm closin' up, mister."

"I just have a quick message to send."

The man, short of stature but sporting a great, unruly bush of black hair on his head, shook his head.

"You'll have to wait until tomorrow," he said. "My missus is waitin' dinner for me."

"Please," Clint said, coming up next to the man, "it's really important. I'll pay you double."

"That's got nothin' to do with it—"

"Triple."

The man stopped short of locking the door and gave Clint a long look.

"It's really that important to you, is it?"

"Yes, sir," Clint said, "it really is."

The man sighed.

"All right, then, but you'll pay me only what the cost is. No more."

"Thank you."

The man opened the door and they both went inside.

"I'm sorry to delay your supper," Clint said.

"A few minutes won't hurt," the man said. Then he looked at Clint and asked, "It *will* only be a few minutes, won't it?"

"Oh, definitely," Clint said. "I know exactly what I want to say."

The man gave Clint a pencil and telegraph pad and waited.

Clint addressed to Bat Masterson, care of Morgan Earp, Tombstone, Arizona. He used Morgan's name because it was he, of the Earp brothers, who was a deputy marshal in Tombstone.

The message itself ran: JIM NEEDS HELP. COME AT ONCE.

He signed: CLINT ADAMS.

"Here it is," he said, pushing it across to the man.

The man nodded, then read to make sure it made sense, and to count the words.

"You're sendin' it to Bat Masterson?"

"That's right."

"Well, why didn't you say so . . . and you're Clint Adams?" This was asked with even more incredulity.

"That's right."

"I'll send it right off, Mr. Adams," the man said nervously.

"How much do I owe you?"

The man stammered out the price, and Clint counted it out.

"Will you be waitin' for an answer?"

"I'll get my answer," Clint said, "when Bat gets here, I hope. Thanks for your help."

"Hey," the man said, "Bat was real good for this town. I'm glad to help him and his brothers. It was a shame what happened to Ed."

"Yes, it was."

"Mr. Adams?" the man said as Clint turned toward the door.

"Yes?"

"You tell the marshal to watch his back until his brother gets here."

Clint turned back to the man.

"What's your name?"

"Henry, sir," the man said, "Henry Collins."

"What do you know, Henry?"

"Nothing, really," Henry said, "but I've heard things."

"What things?"

"Some people are saying that the marshal won't last to the end of the month."

"Who's going to kill him?"

Henry didn't answer right away.

"Henry, earlier tonight the marshal was shot at by his partner, Peacock, and the bartender, Updegraff."

"That's them," Henry said. "Folks are saying Peacock wants the marshal dead. He doesn't want a partner."

Clint frowned. His intention had been to pass through town and just say hello to Jim. Now it looked like he was going to have to stay, at least until Bat arrived.

"Thanks for your help, Henry."

"Sure, Mr. Adams."

"You get that telegraph message off and then go home and have dinner with your wife."

"I'll do that, sir."

Clint left the telegraph office and walked back over to the Lady Gay. He was early, and Miller had apparently gone back to his poker game after he'd left earlier. The man looked up now as Clint entered, nodded, and cashed in his chips. They met at the bar, where a tall, gangly man in his mid-twenties was now tending bar.

"Two beers," Clint said.

"What's goin' on?" Miller asked.

"You really want to know?"

"Why not?" Miller asked. "From the look on your face I'm not gonna be gettin' you near a poker table anytime soon, and the pickin's here are gettin' almost too easy."

The bartender came with their beers and both men picked them up.

"Come on," Miller said, "you might as well tell me what's on your mind."

SIXTEEN

Briefly Clint told Miller what he intended to do, now that he had sent a telegram to Bat Masterson in Tombstone.

"So you have no idea when Bat will arrive?" Miller asked.

"My best guess is five or six days."

"Until then you'll be watchin' Jim's back?"

"Yes."

"And you'll be needin' help?"

"Well . . ."

Miller spread his hands and said, "I'm no gunman, Clint, but I'm here, so if you need my help, I'm offerin' it."

"I appreciate it, Jack. Before you make up your mind, though, maybe you better wait until I introduce the two of you."

"There's no need for that," Miller said. "If I do

this, I'll be doin' it for you."

"I appreciate it," Clint said again.

At that moment Jim Masterson came in the front door. He spotted Clint and walked over to where he was standing with Jack Miller.

"Jim, I want to introduce you to my friend, Jack Miller," Clint said, before the man could speak. "Jack, this is my friend, Jim Masterson."

"I think we got off on the wrong foot," Jim said to Miller. He extended his hand and Miller took it.

"That's all right. It's not an easy job that you have."

"That's the truth," Jim said. He looked at Clint. "I don't know what happened to Peacock and Updegraff. They disappeared."

"What's going on with you and your partner?" Clint asked.

"Ex-partner, thank you."

"Why would he want to shoot it out with you over a bartender?"

"There's more to it than that," Jim said.

"Like what?"

"That's what I want to ask him myself."

"Jim, you need somebody to watch your back," Clint said.

"Are you willing to wear a badge?"

"No, but—"

"Then I'll have to watch my own back, Clint, but thanks."

Jim turned his attention to the bartender and asked for a beer.

"Well, anyway," Clint said, "we're supposed to eat together, right?"

"That's right."

"Do you mind if Jack comes along? It's been a

while since I've seen him, too."

Jim accepted his beer from the bartender and said, "I don't have any objection, Clint. Just let me finish this beer and we'll go over to Delmonico's for steaks."

"That sounds good to me," Clint said.

"Me, too," Miller said.

"Anything to get you out of the saloon and away from the poker table, Mr. Miller," Jim said. "I understand you're killin' us there."

"I'm not doing too badly," Miller said. "Of course, I'd like to get Clint at the poker table."

"That would be interesting to watch," Jim admitted.

"What about you, Marshal?" Jack Miller asked. "Do you play poker?"

"Not me," Jim said, sipping his beer. "My brother Bat is the gambler in our family. Ed and I never really got involved in that."

"I see."

The three men chatted and finished their beers, and when their mugs were empty they left the Lady Gay and walked over to the restaurant.

Clint didn't know why Jim Masterson was being so stubborn about letting him watch his back without a badge. Going to dinner with him, though, was a good way to keep an eye on him. For the rest of the week, until Bat got there, he was going to have to keep coming up with other excuses.

SEVENTEEN

At one point during Clint's story Julia stopped him and asked if he'd mind if she took notes.

"It's not an interview," she said, "but it is an interesting story that you're telling. I mean, it involves the Mastersons as well as your friend Miller."

Clint thought a moment. She *was* trying to help him, and maybe if he let her take notes she'd forget about asking for an interview.

"All right," he said, "go ahead."

That had been earlier, when he first mentioned Bat Masterson. They were still at the restaurant, and Clint decided to have a piece of peach pie with his coffee while Julia hastily jotted down notes from the beginning of the story.

"All right," she'd said then, "you can go ahead."

He then continued from the telegraph office up to

the point where he, Jim, and Jack Miller left the Lady
Gay and started for Delmonico's.

"Wait a minute," she said, interrupting him at that
point. "What does this have to do with Miller saving
your life?"

"I just thought I'd give you the whole story," Clint
said. "After all, we've got time, and you *are* taking
notes . . ."

When he stopped she frowned and asked, "What
is it?"

"Your friend, Lieutenant Milsap, just walked in."

She turned and saw that he was correct.

"Coincidence?" she asked. "Or did he follow us
here?"

"If he followed us," Clint said, "he waited outside
a long time. I didn't see any other restaurants between here and the funeral parlor."

"There aren't any."

As Milsap was led to a table, Clint said, "Well, then,
maybe it really is a coincidence. After all, policemen
have to eat, too, don't they?"

"I've heard that," she said, "but I thought it was
just a rumor."

As the lieutenant sat down at his table he spotted
them and smiled. Julia smiled back and Clint simply
nodded.

The waiter came over and asked, "Anything else,
sir?"

Clint looked at Julia, who said, "I'd like more coffee, and a piece of that peach pie."

"I'll have more coffee, also," Clint said.

"Very good," the waiter said.

"Do you think he'll come over?" Julia asked.

"Maybe not," Clint said. "Maybe he just wants to eat."

"He does want to talk to you, though," she said. "He told me so at the funeral home."

"Did he tell you anything about, uh, Jack's death?" Clint asked.

"I tried to ask him questions, but he's real slippery," she said. "All he said was that he was still looking into it."

Clint looked over at the policeman again. He was studying the menu, not paying them any attention at all.

"I wish I knew how smart he was," Clint said.

"From what I understand he's damned smart."

The waiter returned with Julia's pie and more coffee for both of them.

"Are you going to tell him about your friend?" she asked.

"I don't know," Clint said. "I don't know what I'm going to do yet. I'm still confused. Maybe I'll talk to the family again."

"The two sisters, huh?" Julia said. "Real pretty, especially the younger one."

"Really?" Clint asked. "I sort of preferred Elaine, the older one."

"Oh? You like older women?"

He smiled.

"I like women, Julia, preferably intelligent ones—like you."

"Flatterer," she said. "You'd better go on with your story before the lieutenant decides he wants to interrupt us."

"All right," Clint said, "where was I . . ."

EIGHTEEN

Dodge City
April 11–16

Clint covered the days until Bat's arrival very quickly for Julia. Under one excuse or another he or Miller contrived to be with Jim Masterson as often as possible. During that time they never once saw A. J. Peacock or the man known as Updegraff.

Clint didn't tell Julia about Alice, though. . . .

On the morning of April 16 Clint woke up with Alice Carpenter crouched between his legs. Alice worked at the Lady Gay, and since Clint was spending so much time there she had made a point of getting to know him. Once she realized that he would not pay her to have sex with him she decided she *really* wanted him, so she told him that it would not cost him anything.

That was on April 12, and she had slept in his bed every night since then.

She was an eager sex partner, especially since he was not like the men who paid her. They, she explained, stripped off their clothes, threw themselves on top of her, rutted away for five minutes, splashed out their seed, dressed quickly, and went back to their gambling or drinking.

She told Clint that he was the first man she had ever known who took time with a woman, the first man she had ever been with who was concerned with her pleasure as well as his own.

On this morning she woke him with her eager mouth and avid tongue, and even before he was fully awake he was fully erect and in her mouth. When she had sucked him to the point of no return she released him and gave him one long, loving lick from the base of his penis to the head. Then she sat back and watched as the organ twitched.

"Bitch," he said, laughing so that there was no sting to it.

"If I sit on you now it will be all over," she said teasingly.

"You think."

"I know."

"How do you know?"

"I know men."

"But you've never known a man like me," he said. "I am a man like no other."

She knew he was kidding, but he was also right.

"Wanna see?" she asked.

"I want to see you prove it."

Alice was a plump brunette, with lovely, if somewhat chubby breasts. They were pale and full, the nipples large and sensitive. At the moment they had puckered and hardened, and he knew if he touched them she would catch her breath.

She straddled him, reached between them to hold him steady, and then sat down on him, taking him into her slowly. She sighed when he was all the way in and closed her eyes. He lifted his hands and gently rubbed the palms of his hands over her nipples. Because her eyes were closed and she had not seen what was coming, her breath caught even more than usual and she bit her bottom lip. She began to move on him, her face contorting into a mask of pleasure. Clint was amazed at how many times women in the throes of pleasure looked as if they were in pain.

He slid his hand down her body while she rode him, between her breasts and over her belly and found her moist clitoris. He rubbed it gently with the ball of his thumb. Now she gasped and her body shuddered as waves of pleasure coursed through her.

"You bastard!" she said, opening her eyes. "You just had to prove me wrong, didn't you? You just had to prove that I would come before you."

He reached for her breasts again, sliding his thumbs over the nipples. She went quiet and began to move on him again, faster and faster until he grabbed her hips and lifted his butt off the bed and exploded inside of her with a loud, guttural moan. . . .

"You didn't beat me by much," she said as he dressed.

Lying in the bed with the sheet up to her neck she looked all of eighteen. She *was* young, but he knew she was in her early twenties, at least four years away from eighteen. He tended to stay away from girls in their teens these days. One of them was liable to give him a heart attack.

"I didn't know we were trying to beat each other," he said.

"I might only be twenty-two," she said, "but I've been having sex since I was thirteen. The one thing I've learned is that the bed is a battlefield."

"And you're usually the victor?"

"Just the opposite," she said, chewing her bottom lip. "I've always been the loser . . . until now. It's taken me nine years to find a man I actually enjoy being in bed with."

Dressed, he leaned over her and kissed her.

"Then enjoy it more, Alice. Stop thinking of it as a battle of some kind."

"I try," she said, pressing her cheek into his palm, "I really do."

He left his hand there a moment, then removed it. He took his gun belt from the bedpost and strapped it on.

"When will you be leaving?" she asked.

"Soon, probably."

She sat up and put her arms around her knees.

"I think you've ruined me."

"How?"

"I don't know if I can go back to it after being with you."

"Then don't."

"Oh, sure," she said. "And what am I supposed to do to live?"

"Work in a restaurant," Clint said, "or a dress shop."

"I can't do that."

"Why not?"

"If I was a waitress do you know what kind of tips men would want to give me? If I worked in a dress shop I'd end up in a fitting room with someone's husband while the wife was in the other room trying on a dress."

"It wouldn't have to be that way."

"I don't know any other way."

Now she looked like a very sad little eighteen-year-old, but there wasn't much he could do for her. With a little luck he'd be leaving Dodge City in a day or two, and she'd have to deal with her life on her own.

"You'll have to figure it out for yourself, Alice," he told her.

"I know that," she said. "I always have."

"Do you want to stop—"

"No!" she answered immediately, knowing what he was going to say before he even finished. "No, I'll see you here tonight . . . if you'll have me."

He smiled and said, "See you later."

NINETEEN

As Clint left the Dodge House hotel he saw two men crossing the street toward him. He recognized them as Fred Singer, sheriff of Ford County, and A. B. Webster, the mayor of Dodge. Webster was carrying a shotgun, which was no surprise. He was a "hands on" mayor, the first to volunteer for a posse, not afraid to get his hands dirty.

"Mr. Adams?"

"Mayor," Clint said, "Sheriff, what can I do for you?"

"We'd like to talk to you for a moment," Webster said.

"What about?"

"There's a lot of talk around town about Peacock and Masterson."

"Is there?"

"You know there is," Webster said. "We don't want

a shooting battle in the street, Mr. Adams. Those days are gone in Dodge City."

"What do you want me to do about it?" Clint asked.

Webster looked at Singer, who looked away. Apparently, this was the mayor's idea, and his party.

"We'd like you to leave town."

"What?"

"Uh, leave town."

"Why do you think my leaving town will diffuse the situation?" Clint asked.

"You are seen almost everywhere with Marshal Masterson."

"So?"

"It's . . . inflammatory."

"I'm covering his back, Mayor. If I don't, Peacock and his friend Updegraff are liable to bushwhack him."

"You don't know that."

"Yes, I do," Clint said, "and so do you. That's why you want me to leave."

"I don't understand—"

"You think once I'm gone Peacock will kill Masterson and it will all be over."

"I never—"

Clint looked at Singer and said, "Why are you going along with this, Fred?"

"It's my job," Singer said, but it was one he clearly did not like.

"Mayor," Clint said, "I'm staying until the matter between Jim Masterson and A. J. Peacock is settled, or . . ."

"Or what?"

He'd been about to give away the fact that he'd

sent for Bat Masterson, but he stopped himself in time.

"Or until someone else is here to watch his back."

"Look, Mr. Adams—"

"Mayor, I have nothing else to say to you."

With that Clint stepped down from the boardwalk and walked away, crossing the street.

"Why didn't you say something?" he heard Webster ask Singer.

"Shut up," the sheriff said, sounding weary.

Clint didn't think he had to worry about Singer for the moment. His sympathies were clearly with Masterson. And the mayor would do nothing on his own.

He walked to Delmonico's, where he had taken to having breakfast every day. Sometimes Miller joined him, sometimes Jim Masterson, and sometimes both.

Jim and Jack Miller had slowly become friends. The tension generated by their earlier meeting was gone.

As he entered Delmonico's he saw both men sitting at a table having breakfast.

"You fellas got an early start," he said, joining them.

"We don't have women keeping us in bed until all hours of the morning," Jack Miller pointed out.

"Or mayors and sheriffs stopping us in the street to talk," Jim said.

Clint addressed them in turn.

"You could have a woman if you were nice to them," he said to Miller, "and, Jim, if you want to talk to the mayor and the sheriff I can probably arrange it."

"No, thanks," Jim said.

"What did they want?" Miller asked.

"The mayor is afraid that the streets are going to erupt with lead and that a river of blood will run through the town."

"And?"

"And he asked me to leave."

"What the hell does your bein' here have to do with anythin'?" Jim asked. "This is between me and Peacock and Updegraff."

"If Clint leaves and there's nobody to watch your back," Miller said, "they'll bushwhack you and that will be the end of that. The streets will be safe again."

"What did Fred Singer think of this?" Jim asked.

"Fred's doing his job, but with no great enjoyment." He told them what he'd overheard between the two men as he was walking away.

"Good for Fred," Jim said.

When the waiter came with their food, he had breakfast for the three of them, surprising Clint.

"We ordered for you," Miller said.

"We knew you'd be here," Jim said.

They had ordered three Delmonico steaks with eggs, which was fine with him. There was also already a pot of coffee on the table.

"Bring another pot of coffee, will you?" Clint asked. He wanted it hot.

"Yes, sir."

"So when does he get here?" Jim asked Clint.

"Who?"

"Bat."

Surprised, Clint said, "What makes you think Bat's coming here?"

"Come on, Clint," Jim said. "You can't stay here forever. You must have sent a telegram to Bat, telling him that I needed my back covered."

Clint remained silent.

"Didn't you?"

"Yes."

"So when does he get here?"

"I don't know," Clint said. "Today or tomorrow, I guess. It depends on when he left. That depends on what was happening in Tombstone when he got my message."

"The Earps have been having some trouble there," Jim said.

"I know. Truth is I've been thinking about going to Tombstone, myself."

"They've got Doc Holliday there to help them," Jim said. "Bat probably left soon after he got your message. There's a noon train. He'll probably be on it today or tomorrow. I'll go over to the station today and see if he gets off."

"I'll go with you."

"Me, too," said Miller.

"My nursemaids," Jim said. "I can't wait until Bat gets here, and you two fellas will leave town."

"I kind of like it here," Miller said. "Easy pickings."

"I like it, too."

"You fellas will leave if I have to run you out," Jim said, smiling. "Now eat your breakfast."

TWENTY

After breakfast they all went back to Jim Masterson's office. Jim Masterson was suddenly certain of two things. One, his brother would arrive today or tomorrow. Two, something was going to happen soon.

"Peacock and Updegraff have been hiding too long," he said. "They have to come out soon."

"When they do," Clint asked, "will it be just the two of them, do you think?"

"I don't know," Jim said. "Believe it or not, they have friends."

"Whatever possessed you to become partners with Peacock in the Lady Gay?" Clint asked. The question had been on his mind since Jim Masterson had first told him that he was a partner.

"You're thinkin' about Ed, right?"

Clint nodded.

Jim turned to Miller and said, "My brother Ed was shot in the Lady Gay three years ago. He later died."

"Why would you want to own it, then?"

Jim looked at Miller for a long moment, and then back at Clint.

"I've had it in my mind since Ed was shot that Peacock was behind it, somehow."

"Can you prove it?" Clint asked.

"No. That was why when I heard Peacock was in financial trouble I offered to buy half of the Lady Gay. He needed the money or he would have lost the place completely, so we became partners."

"Not a partnership made in heaven, I'm sure," Clint said.

"No. We fought at every turn and then a few weeks ago he hired Updegraff against my will."

"You think he brought Updegraff in to kill you?"

"Seems that way, don't it?" Jim asked. "Or at least to back his play."

"And then they muffed it," Miller said.

"Right."

"What if they've left town?" Miller asked.

"I don't think so," Jim said. "If something happens to me Peacock still owns the Lady Gay."

"But if they kill you, they'll be arrested," Miller said.

"Only if it can be proved that they did it," Jim said. "If they bushwhack me and get away with it . . ." He spread his hands.

"Well, they're not going to bushwhack you," Clint said, "not if we can help it."

Jim made two pots of coffee and by the time they drank it all it was nearly twelve.

"I've got a good feeling," Jim Masterson said as

they left his office. "I feel that Bat will be on this train."

"Have you had those kinds of feelings before?" Miller asked. "Are you and your brother close?"

"We're close, but no, I haven't felt this before."

Clint hoped that Jim was right. He'd grown tired of Dodge City, tired of waiting for something to happen. It was time to let Bat and Jim handle the problem as a family, and get on the trail again.

They got to the station at five minutes to twelve, and they could hear the train whistle in the distance.

"It's gonna be a couple of minutes early," Jim said.

"I hope he's on it," Clint said.

"Tired of watchin' after me, huh?" Jim asked.

"Hey," Clint said, "I've got a life, you know."

The train came into sight and in seconds it was rumbling into the station. As passengers got off, the three men looked both ways and it was finally Clint who spotted Bat, impeccably dressed as usual, sporting a bowler hat.

"Your feeling was right, Jim," Clint called out. "There he is."

Jim and Miller turned and looked down the track. As all three men watched, Bat Masterson saw them, waved, and started toward them, carrying a small carpetbag in his left hand. The three stood their ground and waited for him to reach them, but before he did they saw Bat draw his gun, point it in their direction, and fire.

"What the hell—" Clint said.

TWENTY-ONE

It became immediately apparent that Bat was firing at someone behind them. As Clint heard the other shots being fired, he threw himself to the ground, rolling, and came up on one knee with his gun out. There were three men standing on the platform, firing at them. Clint didn't know where Miller or Jim Masterson were, and he didn't have time to check. He fired once and a man fell.

Now there were more shots from his side, being fired at the two remaining men. He watched as their bodies jerked and spasmed as a hail of lead struck them, and then they were on the ground.

He stood up and looked around for the others, hoping no one was hurt.

Bat Masterson had dropped to one knee and was now standing up.

Jim Masterson had dropped into a prone position on his belly.

Jack Miller had taken cover behind a barrel.

All four men regained their feet and came together in the center of the platform.

"Everyone all right?" Clint asked.

No one was hit.

Bat took hold of Jim by the arms and said, "Good to see you, Jim."

"Thanks for comin', Bat."

"Not that you'd wire your big brother on your own," Bat said. He turned to Clint and extended his hand. The two men shook warmly.

"Good to see you, Bat."

"Bat, this is Jack Miller," Jim said. "He's with us."

"I know you," Bat said, shaking hands with Miller. "Denver, right? A poker tournament?"

"That was some years ago, Bat," Miller said. "I'm surprised that you remember."

"I have a good memory for faces," Bat said. "Speakin' of faces, why don't we go and make sure those three fellas are dead?"

The four of them walked to the bodies together and checked them.

"This one's dead," Bat said.

"So's this one," Miller said.

"And this one," Jim added.

"Do you know any of them, Jim?"

"Not this one," Jim said of the one he'd checked. He walked to where Bat was, and then over to Miller.

"Bat, isn't this . . . ?"

Bat walked over and looked at the man.

"That's Andy Barlow."

"That's who it is," Jim said, snapping his fingers.

"I thought I recognized him."

"Who is he?" Clint asked.

"He works for Peacock."

"Ah," Bat said, "and where is Peacock?"

"And Updegraff," Miller said.

"Who?" Bat asked.

Briefly, Jim explained to his brother about Peacock and Updegraff.

"I don't know why you bothered getting involved with Peacock, Jim."

"We talked about it, Bat."

"Yeah, yeah, I know," Bat said, "Ed . . ."

"I think we should get off this platform," Miller suggested. "We're out in the open, and we still don't know where those other two are."

"I think that's a good idea," Clint said.

"Let's go to my office," Jim said. "If they want us, they can come for us there."

As they started walking Bat said, "Well, we've got one advantage over them."

"We don't know how many of *them* there are," Miller pointed out.

"Maybe not," Bat said, "but they didn't expect me to be here, either."

TWENTY-TWO

They started their walk from the train station to the marshal's office, going right down Main Street. They walked back-to-back, each facing a different direction, like some eight-legged creature, covering each other's backs.

"Somethin's gonna happen," Jim Masterson said. "The street's too empty."

"Keep a sharp eye out," Bat said. "A. J. Peacock's idea of a fair fight is an ambush."

"As we've already seen," Miller said.

Just as he spoke a bullet kicked up some dirt in front of them, just a split second before the report of the shot reached them.

"Scatter!" Clint shouted, as more shots rained down on them from rooftops.

As they dove for cover Clint heard the unmistakable sound of lead striking flesh, and he wondered who was hit. Just seconds later he felt the burning sensation in his leg, and the wetness of his own blood. That answered his question.

He wondered who else might have been hit.

He found cover behind a nearby horse trough and then examined his leg. The bullet appeared to have creased him and gone right on by, and not through.

There was still shooting from the rooftops, and a couple of bullets splashed into the water of the trough. Pinned down, but momentarily safe, Clint decided to wait out the barrage, which could not keep up forever.

At the moment that Clint had shouted to the others everyone did exactly what he'd said—they scattered.

Jim Masterson ducked into a doorway.

Bat Masterson sought cover behind some barrels in front of the hardware store.

Jack Miller found refuge behind a nearby buckboard.

All were pinned down as the firing continued from the rooftops. Apparently, A. J. Peacock had enlisted a lot of help for this attack, starting at the train station. Maybe he'd hoped that if they managed to avoid being killed at the station they would be lulled into a false sense of security and be easy targets on the street. They might have been easy targets if someone had not fired prematurely, and missed, thereby warning them and saving their lives.

As abruptly as it had begun the firing stopped. Clint decided not to call out to the others, on the off chance that someone had managed to find cover out of sight of the shooters.

Clint took the opportunity to peek up over the trough at the roof across the street. He had the impression that they'd been fired on from both sides. He was lying on the left side of the street, looking up at the rooftops on the right. That meant that he was out of sight of whoever was on the roof on his side of the street. Gun in hand he tried to spot someone across the street.

"Bat!"

Clint heard the voice and immediately identified it as that of Jim Masterson. Apparently, his concern for his brother was overriding his good sense.

"Bat! Are you all right?"

Clint listened, but Bat did not respond. Either he was hit and down, or he simply did not want to give away his location. Clint decided to believe the latter was true.

Jim seemed to realize this and fell silent.

Clint continued to watch the roof across the way. The shooters were probably reloading, and when they were ready would start firing again. He might only get one shot, and he wanted to make it count . . .

At this point in the story Julia Tisdale interrupted him.

"You were shot, right?"

"That's right."

"Didn't you need medical attention?"

"The wound wasn't serious."

"But how did you know that?"

Clint found the question naive, but then he was talking to someone who had never been away from

Chicago, who had probably never been shot *at* in her life, let alone shot.

"I've been shot enough times, Julia, to know when I'm seriously injured or not."

Her eyes widened.

"How many times have you been shot?"

"That's not important to this story," Clint said. "That's the kind of question you would ask in an interview."

Sheepishly, she admitted he was right.

"Shall I continue?" he asked.

"Just a moment."

While she was busily jotting something down Clint looked over at Lieutenant Milsap, who had finished his meal and was having some coffee. The policeman chose that moment to look over at them and caught Clint's eye. The two men nodded at each other, Clint hoping that the man would not take it as an invitation to walk over and join them.

"All right," Julia said, "you can go on."

"There's not much more to tell . . ."

TWENTY-THREE

Clint waited patiently for his shot. The men had plenty of time to reload, and he thought they should reappear at any moment. Finally, he was rewarded for his patience. On the rooftop across from him two men appeared, aiming their rifles. Before they could get off a shot Clint fired. He must have struck one of the men in the head. A rifle fell from the roof and struck the ground, discharging. The man slumped out of sight, and his partner along with him, probably in shock.

Clint chose that moment to move. He didn't know which roof their assailants were occupying on his side of the street, but he now knew where they were across the way. He stood up and started running across the street, hoping to catch everyone by surprise.

"Clint! Here!" Jim Masterson shouted, but Clint ignored him and kept running until he reached an alley. He'd caught everyone flat-footed with his shot and his run, and not a shot had been fired at him.

When Bat Masterson saw Clint start his run he knew it was his chance, as well. The shooters were caught flat-footed, and by the time they recovered, Clint was safely across the street. The last thing they'd expect would be for someone else to try the same thing.

As soon as Clint was safely in the alley Bat reacted immediately. He left the cover of the barrels and sprinted across the street.

Only this time the shooters were quicker to react.

From his new vantage point Clint could see the men on the roof on the other side of the street. He also saw that Bat Masterson was trying the same thing he tried, only the shooters were quicker to react this time.

"Cover him!" Clint shouted and started shooting. Jim Masterson and Jack Miller followed his example.

The two men across the street withdrew their rifles and ducked for cover.

On the other side one man was still staring at the dead body of the other man, who had been hit square in the forehead by Clint's bullet. The man couldn't take his eyes off the bullet hole, which was almost like a third eye. Consequently he never took a shot at Bat Masterson, even though he would have been the only man with clear aim.

Bat made it safely across the street.

The man didn't know that, but he made a snap decision of his own.

• • •

Jim Masterson was confused. He'd seen Clint sprint across the street to his side, and then his brother run across to the other. What the hell was he supposed to do?

"Miller? You okay?" he called.

"I'm not hit," Miller replied.

They were close enough together that the men on the rooftops would not hear their conversation.

"What the hell do we do now?" Jim asked.

"We wait, I guess."

"For what?"

"Obviously Clint and Bat have something in mind. Let's let them play it out, and be ready to help if we have to."

"Shit," Jim said. He was the law, not Clint, and not Bat. This was his responsibility. Updegraff and Peacock were his business to take care of.

He was about to stand up when the men across the street got back up and started firing at him. He managed to get a look at them before ducking for cover. One he didn't recognize, but he was sure the other was A. J. Peacock.

The bastard!

"Jack," he called. "Cover me."

"Wha—" Miller said, but before he could say anything else Jim Masterson was running across the street the way his brother had gone.

Miller stood up to cover and saw Jim flinch as a bullet must have struck him. Miller started firing, but had to stop when his six-gun ran out of live shells. The two men across the street had rifles, and they were able to continue firing. Jim Masterson had made it across, probably wounded, but still on his feet.

Miller reloaded, then decided that while Jim was backing up his brother, he was left with the task of backing up Clint Adams.

Only there was now no one to cover his move.

Clint worked his way around to the back of the building the men were on. Near as he could figure there were four of them—three depending on how badly hurt the man he had hit was. He was moving quickly, hoping to find a way to the roof before the men could collect themselves, or get away.

Across the street Bat had also worked himself around to the back of the building the shooters were on. He was hoping to find a way to the roof, and when he reached the rear of the building he found that he was in luck. There was a stairway leading almost all the way up. When he got to the top all he'd have to do was stand on the railing, reach up, and pull himself onto the roof. Unfortunately, that would make him pretty vulnerable if the men who were already up there spotted him.

He heard someone behind and turned quickly, his gun ready.

"Jesus, don't shoot," Jim Masterson said. "I've already been shot enough times today."

"You're hit?" Bat asked his brother.

Jim nodded.

"How bad?"

Jim indicated the hole in his left arm.

"I'll need a doctor when we're done," he said, "but I'll be all right."

"This is the building they're on," Bat said. "I'm going up."

"Peacock's up there," Jim said. "I want him, Bat. I'm going."

"No, I'll go. You're hurt."

"This is my fight, Bat, and my job."

"I can't say nothin' about your job, Jim," Bat said, "but you're my brother. If it's your fight, it's mine, too. Nothin' you can say will change that."

Jim hesitated a moment, then said, "All right, then let's both go up."

When Bat looked up at the top of the stairs he saw a pair of legs hanging from the roof.

"Well, well," he said to Jim, "looks like we won't have to go up and get 'em. They're comin' down."

"Let's take cover," Jim said, "and wait for 'em."

TWENTY-FOUR

The man with Peacock was the first to reach the ground. Peacock himself was just dropping down from the roof to the landing. Bat wanted to tell his brother to wait, but Jim, impatient as usual, stepped out of hiding as soon as the first man's feet touched dirt.

"Hold it!"

The man turned and went for his gun immediately. Jim, his gun already out, fired once. The bullet struck the man in the chest, driving him back a few steps before he fell to the ground, dead.

At the top of the landing Peacock had seen what was going on. His head was whipping around, his eyes frantically looking for a way out.

"Don't try it, A. J.," Bat called out.

Peacock looked up and decided to try to get back

on the roof. He jumped, but missed and staggered, almost falling.

"Peacock!" Jim Masterson shouted. "You're under arrest. Come on down."

Peacock sneaked one look back down at the Mastersons, then climbed on the stair railing to reach the roof.

"Where's he gonna go once he gets on the roof?" Bat asked, shaking his head.

"He ain't gettin' on the roof," Jim said.

"If you shoot him now you'll hit him in the ass," Bat said.

"Serves him right," Jim said. "He was always an asshole, anyway."

"Jim—"

Jim pointed his gun and fired. The bullet struck Peacock in the butt just seconds before he would have safely been on the roof. The impact of the bullet lifted him up and onto the roof.

"Great," Bat said, staring at his brother. "Now we've got to go up and get him."

Clint came around behind the building he thought the men were on and studied it for a way up. There was no way on the outside that he could see, unless he had a ladder, which he didn't. He was going to have to go inside.

Just as he was going to do so he spotted something. It looked like a man's foot up on the roof. Was one of them actually going to try to climb down?

"Hold it!" Clint shouted. The man's foot didn't move. "I said—"

"You hold it," another man's voice said.

Clint froze. Updegraff had stepped out of the back

door and was pointing a gun at him. He had come out while Clint was talking to the foot on the roof, the foot that probably belonged to a dead man.

He'd been suckered.

"Drop the gun, Adams," the man said.

"I can't," Clint said.

"Why not?"

"If I do I'm dead."

"If you try to turn I'll kill you, anyway," Updegraff said. "I've got my finger on the trigger."

"Well," Clint said, "I'd rather die that way."

"It'll be my pleasure—"

"Hold it!" someone yelled for the third time in two minutes.

It was Jack Miller. Updegraff whirled around, but before he could squeeze the trigger Clint turned and fired. Updegraff was slammed back into the door by Clint's shot, and then slid down to the ground where he slumped motionless.

"You saved my life!" Miller said.

"Looked to me like you saved mine," Clint said.

"It's your bullet in Updegraff. I owe you."

"Let's call it even," Clint said.

"That was very close," Julia said.

"Too close," Clint said.

Julia finished writing and looked up.

"And that was the last time you saw him?"

"That was it."

"What happened to the Mastersons?"

"Jim stayed in Dodge for a while then moved on. Bat kept moving on for a while. He was in Denver last time I saw him."

"And Jack Miller ended his life here in Chicago," she said.

"Yes . . . no! No, he didn't." For a moment it seemed they'd both forgotten why they were there. "The man in the coffin is not Jack."

"How do you propose to prove it?"

"I don't know . . . I suppose I'd better talk to the family."

"And tell them what?"

"I don't know," he said. "I can't very well tell them that the man in the box is not their son, or brother."

"And what about the lieutenant?" she asked.

"What about him?"

"Do you intend to tell him that the dead man is not Jack Miller?"

"He might very well *be* Jack Miller," Clint said. "The man I knew may be the one who is not Jack Miller."

"This is all very confusing," Julia said.

"And that may be the only thing we know for certain."

Julia turned her head and said, "No, it's not."

"What else do we know?"

"We know that Lieutenant Milsap is coming over to our table."

TWENTY-FIVE

Clint looked up just as Milsap reached their table.

"Do you mind if I sit a minute?" he asked, without preamble.

"We were just about to leave, Lieutenant," Clint said.

The man sat anyway.

"It won't take long."

"I really have to get back to work, Lieutenant," Julia said.

"Well, Miss Tisdale," Milsap said, "the truth is you can leave if you like. I'd just like to speak with Mr. Adams for a moment or two."

Clint looked at Julia and said, "Go ahead, Julia. I'll talk to you later."

Julia quickly scribbled on a piece of paper and handed it to Clint, then hurried out.

"Why don't we get some more coffee," Milsap suggested.

"I thought this wasn't going to take too long," Clint said.

"Are you telling me you don't like my company, Mr. Adams?"

"I'd never say that, Lieutenant."

Milsap waved at the waiter, who obviously knew he was a policeman and came running over.

"More coffee."

"Yessir!"

"Well," Milsap said, "did you have a pleasant meal with Miss Tisdale?"

"It was fine."

"She's a lovely young woman."

"Yes, she is."

"It can't be easy for a woman in the newspaper business."

"Is this what you wanted to talk to me about, Lieutenant? The problem women have with careers?"

Milsap laughed.

"No, not at all," he said. "I'm just . . . warming up."

"I think we're warmed up. What is it you really want to talk about?"

"Well, how about . . . murder."

"Are you telling me that Jack Miller was murdered?"

"Yes, that's what I'm telling you."

"None of the newspapers say that."

"I know. We've kept it out of the newspapers."

"Why?"

Milsap hesitated, then sat back when the waiter returned with another pot of coffee. He started to pour and the lieutenant stopped him.

"We can do that."

"Yes, sir," the man said. He put the pot down and retreated.

Milsap poured before continuing.

"The Millers are a very prominent Chicago family, did you know that?"

"No, I didn't."

"Really? You were friends with the deceased and you didn't know that?"

"He never told me much about his family."

"Well, they are prominent, and I'm getting pressure to solve this murder."

"And why are you telling me this?"

"Because I know who you are."

"You do."

"Yes."

"And what's that got to do with anything?"

"I . . . need your help."

Clint wondered when and where he'd gotten this reputation as some sort of detective.

"I would think you'd have a lot of men working on this case."

"I do," Milsap said, "and I have. What I need is a fresh outlook—your outlook."

Clint had to admit he'd never expected this. Just in his short acquaintance with the lieutenant the man did not strike him as the type to ask for outside help.

"I'm putting my cards on the table, Adams," Milsap said. "I need help."

Clint sipped his coffee for a few moments and then made up his mind.

"If I'm going to work with you," Clint said, "I have to tell you something."

"What?"

Clint hesitated, then said, "It's going to sound crazy."

"Let me be the judge of that," Milsap said. "If it has something to do with this case, I want to hear it."

"All right," Clint said, leaning forward. "The man in the coffin in that funeral parlor is not the Jack Miller I knew."

Milsap waited a few heartbeats and then said, "What?"

"I mean, his name may be Jack Miller, but he's not the Jack Miller I know."

Milsap took a few moments to absorb that and then said, "You mean you came to the wrong Jack Miller's funeral."

"I'd like it if that were the case, Lieutenant."

"And why isn't it?"

"Because I got a telegram telling me about Jack Miller's death in Chicago."

"So somebody wanted you here."

"Right."

"Who?"

"I don't know," Clint said. "The telegram wasn't signed."

"Did you mention this to anyone at the funeral home?" Milsap asked.

"No."

"What do you intend to do now?"

"I don't know," Clint said. "I thought maybe I'd go and talk to the family. Maybe they know the man I knew as Jack Miller."

"Just how well did you know this man?"

Clint took a few moments to explain to the lieutenant—in much less detail then he had with Julia—

about his friendship with Jack Miller.

"Well," Milsap said, "this is odd."

"Yes, it is."

"Did the Millers accept you as Jack's friend?"

"Yes."

"Well, then, maybe you better go ahead and talk to them."

"And what will you do?"

"Let me have that telegram," Milsap said, "and I'll see if I can find the office it was sent from. Maybe we can get a description of the man who sent it."

"All right," Clint said. It was a damned good idea, and one the lieutenant would have more luck with than he would. He took out the telegram and handed it over. Milsap took a moment to read it, then tucked it away inside his jacket.

"I'll get on this tomorrow morning."

"I'll start on the family tomorrow," Clint said. "They've invited me to the house tomorrow after the funeral."

"Good. We'll have to stay in touch on this, Adams."

"Why don't you call me Clint, Lieutenant," he suggested. "It sounds more like we're working together."

"All right, Clint," Milsap said, "my name is John."

Clint nodded, but thought that he'd probably continue to call the man "Lieutenant"—just for a while longer.

Clint and Lieutenant John Milsap left the restaurant together. Seeing this the man standing across the street sank back into the shadows, not wanting to be seen by either of them. The two stopped just outside to exchange a few more words, and then walked in separate directions. The man thought that the two looked friendly—too friendly for men who had just met hours earlier.

What was going on?

It was getting late, and almost dark, so the man could not imagine where else Clint Adams could be going now but back to his hotel. He decided to play this hunch and give Clint Adams lots of room this time.

TWENTY-SIX

When Clint got back to his hotel he was surprised to find Julia Tisdale waiting in the lobby. She approached him quickly—so quickly he thought she was going to run into him.

"Well?"

"Well what?"

"What did he want?"

"I thought you had work to do?"

"I do," she said. "This *is* work."

"Oh."

"What happened?"

"Well," he said, looking around, "let's find someplace to talk. How about a drink?"

"I don't think I could put another bit of food or drink in my body," she said. "Why don't we go someplace else to talk? Someplace private?"

"Where did you have in mind?"

"How about your room?"

He hesitated, then said, "Are you sure about that?"

"Why not?" she asked. "Are you worried about your reputation?"

"It wasn't *my* reputation I was worried about."

"Don't worry about mine," she said. "I'm a news-paperwoman, remember?"

"What does that mean?"

"It means I would do anything for a story," she said. "*That's* my reputation."

"I see."

"Shall we go?"

He shrugged and said, "Why not?"

Outside the front door of the hotel, looking in, the man was pleased that he'd been right about Clint Adams. He watched Clint talk to the woman from the *Tribune*, and then they both proceeded upstairs.

Which, knowing Clint Adams, was no surprise at all.

Clint unlocked the door to his room and let Julia go in ahead of him.

"Okay, what did he have to say?" she asked, before he could even lock the door.

There was one armchair in the room, and then the bed was the only other place to sit. She nonchalantly sat on the bed, so he took the chair and sat facing her. He told her about his conversation with Milsap and ended with how they were going to work to-gether.

"I'm impressed," she said when he was done. "From everything I've heard about Milsap he doesn't work with anybody. He doesn't even work with any of the other policemen."

"Well, I think this arrangement is less due to me and more due to him."

"What do you mean?"

"He's worried about this case," Clint said. "My guess is he'd do almost anything to solve it, because the Miller family is so prominent. That sort of puts him in the same category as you, doesn't it?"

"Except for one thing," she said.

"What's that?"

She surprised him by standing up, walking to the chair, and plopping herself down in his lap, her legs straddling him.

"He doesn't kiss as good as I do."

With that she kissed him, her mouth forcing his lips open, her tongue invading his mouth. It was a hot kiss that got hotter. He pulled her shirt out from her skirt and slid his hands beneath it. Her skin was firm and smooth. There wasn't an ounce of fat on her, and yet her breasts felt very soft and ample against his chest.

"Oooh," she said, "that was nice. I didn't surprise you?"

"Yes," he said, "you most certainly did."

"Oh . . . well, good."

"Do you mind if I ask why?"

"Are you attracted to me?"

"Very much so."

"And to the Miller girls?"

He hesitated, then said, "Yes."

"Well, I just thought I should make my move before they made theirs. Do you mind?"

"Not if you don't mind if I make a move back."

She smiled and said, "I was hoping you would."

That said, he stood up, lifting her with him and carrying her to the bed. He set her on it gently and then lay beside her. He kissed her, sliding his hand beneath her shirt again. He slid it all the way up so he could kiss the smooth flesh of her stomach.

"This is not part of the interview, is it?" he asked, his mouth on her flesh.

"Shut up and undress me. . . ."

TWENTY-SEVEN

Clint discovered that he was right. Julia's body was devoid of any fat, and yet she still had full, firm breasts. He explored her with his mouth and his hands and told her that her body was phenomenal. She thanked him and proceeded to prove that she was phenomenal in bed.

Later, when she was sitting astride him, with his penis buried deep inside of her, he marveled at how firm her breasts were. They were like two ripe melons, and yet there was no sag to them. He held them and squeezed them and bit them, all to her delight while she rode him up and down. When he'd met her, fully dressed and in her work environment, there had been no hint that she would become this eager, uninhibited creature in bed. Neither was there any indication that she would have a body this marvelous.

She was one of the few women in his life who had ever surprised him . . . and he liked it.

"Surprised you, didn't I?" she asked.

"I thought we'd already established that."

They were lying side by side on their backs with the sheet over them. He could feel the heat from her body, and he was still semi-aroused, even though they had made love twice.

"I mean I really surprised you."

"Yes," he said. "You must be used to that."

"To what?"

"Surprising men."

"I haven't been with a lot of men."

He remained silent.

"All right, I've been with *some* men, and yes, they've been surprised. Why is that?"

"It could be that you're an entirely different person with your clothes off."

"I have to be a different person when I'm working," she said. "It's the only way I can get anyone to take me seriously, by *being* serious."

"If it works, then keep doing it."

"It's not the real me, though. Sometimes it's hard being somebody else."

"I know how that feels," Clint said. "People always want me to be someone else, the someone they've heard of and read about."

"Well, then being interviewed by me would fix all that, wouldn't it?"

"Would it?"

"Of course. I would write about the real you."

"Do you think you know the real me?"

"Well, no, but that's why you'd let me interview

you, so you could tell me about the real you."

"And how long would that take?"

"I don't know. How long are you going to be here?"

"Not long, I hope," he said.

"That's flattering."

"Let me rephrase that, then," he said. "I never had any intention of staying any longer than it took to pay my respects to a dead friend."

"And now he's not your friend."

"Or he's not dead."

"Whichever," she said. She got up on one elbow and looked down at him. "What are you going to do?"

"Well, I'll go to the funeral tomorrow, and then to the house after that."

"And then?"

"And then I guess I'll just make it up as I go along."

"And what is the lieutenant going to do?"

"He's going to see if he can find out who sent me the telegram in Texas."

"Somebody wanted you here for a reason," she said. "It would be nice if we knew what that reason was."

"Yes," he said, "it would be."

Abruptly she said, "I have to go." She tossed back the bed covers and stood up. It was remarkable to watch her get dressed. He was fascinated by the way her muscles played beneath her firm flesh. Her breasts hardly swayed as she moved.

"How do you do that?" he asked.

"What?" She sat on the bed to pull on her boots.

"Get your body in that condition and then keep it that way."

"Oh, it won't be like this forever," she said, standing up. "I just get a lot of exercise. I'm always on the go, and I don't eat that much."

"I'll bet other women would pay you if you could teach them how to do it."

"I can't teach them to be me," Julia said. "This is just a result of the way my body works, Clint."

"Well, it's wonderful the way your body works, Miss Tisdale."

She leaned over and kissed him, looked in his eyes and said, "That's something else I should have told you."

"What?"

"It's not 'Miss' Tisdale."

More slowly he said, "What?"

"It's Mrs. Tisdale."

He hesitated, then said, "You're a widow?"

She shook her head.

"Divorced?"

"No."

"You're . . . married?"

"I'm afraid so."

She picked up her belongings and headed for the door quickly.

"Wait," he said, "why didn't you tell—"

"Gotta go," she said, opening the door. "I'll meet you tomorrow for lunch, before you go to the funeral."

"Julia!"

"Bye," she said, and was out the door, closing it quickly behind her.

TWENTY-EIGHT

The next morning Clint had a leisurely breakfast in the dining room of the hotel while reading the *Chicago Tribune*. He looked for something with Julia's byline, but apparently she didn't have anything in this edition.

He was still thinking about that bombshell she had dropped on him on her way out of his room late last night. Clint tried never to sleep with married women. He didn't have any trouble finding bed partners, so it wasn't necessary to take someone else's. She was going to have some explaining to do when she showed up this afternoon.

He had to admit, though, that he was impressed with her. It was not only his opinion after spending most of the day—and night—with her, but the fact that there was nothing in the newspaper that morning. He had to admit that his distrust of newspaper people had made him sure that something would appear in the paper under the guise of an "interview." But no, she had surprised him. Apparently she was truly going to wait for his okay to print something. Either that or she figured this Jack Miller business had the makings of a great story, and she didn't want to ruin it.

If that was it then she was just angling for the better story. He preferred to think that she was being honorable—rare for someone in her business.

Since there wasn't anything in the paper by Julia Tisdale there was nothing else of interest to him, so he folded up the paper and set it aside. He was about to signal the waiter for another pot of coffee when he noticed the woman standing at the entrance of the dining room. She could have been there for any reason, but when she saw him and started toward him he knew that *he* was the reason.

"Mr. Adams," she said. "I'm glad I found you. May I sit?"

"Certainly, Miss Miller."

She sat and said, "Please, you were a friend of Jack's. Call me Elaine."

"All right," he said, "and you call me Clint. Would you like some coffee?"

"Please."

He signaled the waiter for another pot and another cup.

He looked across the table at the oldest of Jack Miller's sisters. Once again he was struck by her beauty, even in her black mourning clothes. She did not seem to be forty yet—although it was probably a year or two off. Nevertheless, she was an extremely attractive woman—not as beautiful as her younger sister, but with seemingly more character in her appearance. She would continue to be attractive for years to come, while Evelyn, once her apparent beauty faded, would be just that, a faded beauty.

The waiter appeared with the fresh pot and poured them each a cup.

"What can I do for you, Elaine?"

"I wanted to talk to you about my brother."

"What about him?"

"Well . . . I doubt that you know this, but he did not die of natural causes."

"Oh, no?"

"It's being kept quiet," she said, "but he was killed."

"How?"

"Murdered."

"In what fashion?"

"Well . . . we're not yet sure about that. There were no obvious wounds that I could see."

"The police allowed you to examine the body?"

"Well, I had to identify him," she said, "but I saw him even before that. You see, I found him."

"That must have been terrible for you."

"It was," she said.

"Where did you find him?"

"In a hotel."

"What was he doing in a hotel?"

"Meeting me."

Clint was confused.

"Why were you two meeting in a hotel?" he asked. "Couldn't you talk at home?"

Elaine studied him for a few moments.

"Can I trust you, Clint?"

"To do what?"

"To keep what I tell you a secret, just between you and me."

"Sure," Clint said, "if that's what you want."

"That's what I want."

"All right, then."

"I—I saw you with that newspaperwoman at the funeral parlor yesterday."

"Julia Tisdale? Where do you know her from?"

"She came to talk to us after Jack was killed. You won't tell her what I tell you, will you?"

"No," Clint said. "If you want it to be just between us, that's the way it will be."

She sipped her coffee, then sat back, staring at him. She seemed relieved to be able to have someone to talk to. At that moment, though, Clint noticed two men come into the room. One of them he recognized from the funeral home. It was Earl Miller, Elaine's brother.

"Isn't that Earl?"

Suddenly, Elaine didn't look relieved. She looked frightened. Why would her own brother frighten her?

Earl Miller saw them and came walking over. The other man stood by the doorway. Clint noticed that Earl was not armed, but the man by the door was.

"There you are, Elaine."

She looked up at her brother.

"Earl, I—"

"Been here long?" he asked. "Good morning, Mr. Adams."

"Morning, Earl," Clint said. "Actually, your sister and I haven't had much time to talk yet. She just got here."

"That's too bad," Earl said. He had his hand on Elaine's shoulder and Clint could see that he was exerting some pressure there.

"Mother sent me to get you, Elaine."

"Earl, I—"

"She needs you." Earl slid his hand down to his sister's elbow and then lifted her from her chair that way. She wasn't forced to her feet, but she didn't seem all that willing, either. Clint was completely confused, and unsure about what to do.

"Elaine—" he said, but Earl cut him off.

"You and my sister can have your talk another time, Mr. Adams," he said. "My mother really needs her, right now."

Clint looked at Elaine, who still looked frightened, but she wasn't asking for help.

"Come to the funeral later, Clint?" she asked as her brother led her away. "At three? And the house afterward?"

"I'll be there. . . . "

He watched as she and Earl reached the other man, who took Elaine's other elbow, and then they were gone.

TWENTY-NINE

Clint was left to wonder what it was Elaine Miller was going to tell him that was such a secret. Why was she meeting her brother in a hotel? Did they have some big secret even the rest of the family didn't know about? And why was she so obviously afraid of her brother Earl? Should he have gotten in between brother and sister and not have let Earl take her out? If she didn't want to go with Earl wouldn't she have said something?

Clint finished the second pot of coffee and then paid his bill and left the dining room. He went out the front door, walked along Michigan Avenue until he reached Rush Street and then turned there. Rush Street seemed to be dominated by restaurants and saloons and clubs, but at this time of day most of them were not open yet. At night, when the sun went down, Rush Street came alive. He'd been to Chicago before and had enjoyed the pleasures that Rush Street had to offer, but this visit was not for that. This was not a pleasure trip, but neither had it been the kind of trip he'd expected. He'd intended to be in and out, paying his respects, and now there were mysteries to be solved. Why were there always problems or mysteries to be solved? On the other hand, what would he do if they suddenly disappeared from his life?

He walked for a long time on Rush Street, then walked back. Julia Tisdale would be coming by at lunchtime to talk to him before he left for the funeral home. Meanwhile, he wondered how Milsap was doing trying to track down the person who sent the telegram.

As he approached the hotel he scolded himself for not having asked the lieutenant where his office was. Then again, the man probably didn't want him to know where the office was, just as he didn't want anyone to know that he had enlisted help outside of the police department.

By the time he got back to the hotel the bar in the saloon had opened. It was still a little early for him, but he decided to kill some time over a beer.

He had almost finished the beer when Julia appeared in the doorway. Since he was the only man in the room, except for the bartender, she spotted him immediately.

"A little early for a beer, isn't it?" she asked, sitting opposite him.

"I'm just killing time."

"You don't have a drinking problem, do you?"

"No."

"Think I can get some coffee here?"

"I'll get it."

He went to the bar and came back with a cup of coffee. He set it down in front of her and sat down again.

"Are you angry with me?" she asked.

"Shouldn't I be?"

"I suppose so."

"Are you still living with your husband?"

"Yes. But he's frequently out of town. He travels a lot."

"So why don't you wear a ring? Why do you let the lieutenant call you 'Miss Tisdale'?"

"As a female reporter, I've found I have more leverage if men think I'm single."

"Do you do this sort of thing a lot?"

She gave him a quick look and said, "No, I do not."

"Then what was last night all about?"

"I don't know," she said. "I was just . . . attracted to you. I couldn't help it."

"I suppose I should be flattered, shouldn't I?"

"I don't . . . yes, I suppose . . . Oh, I don't know . . . I find this very confusing, Clint."

"I'm glad to hear that."

"Why don't we just say that it will never happen again and let it go at that, all right?"

"I suppose so . . ."

"I mean, it's not like you're in love with me or anything like that, right?"

"Right."

"And I'm not in love with you."

"That's good."

"So we can get on with business, then."

"Right."

"Have you talked with Lieutenant Milsap today?"

"No," he said, "but I had another visitor today."

"Oh? Who?"

"Elaine Miller."

"Ah, was that the older blonde or the younger blonde?" Julia asked.

"The older one—although she's not that old. Maybe thirty-eight, forty."

"Is that the age you like them?"

"Julia—"

"Where did this conversation take place? In your room?"

"Well," Clint said, "so much for getting back to business."

She closed her eyes and sat back.

"I'm sorry," she said, "I'm sorry, that was uncalled-for."

They sat there for a few moments in silence before she spoke again.

"What did she want?"

"That's just it," Clint said. "I never did find out. Her brother came to get her."

"Her brother?"

"Earl," Clint said. "I met him at the funeral home."

"Oh, yes," Julia said. "I remember two men, one older and one younger. The younger one would have been Earl."

"Yes."

"How did he know she was here?"

"I don't know," Clint said. "He came walking in just a little after she did, saying that her mother needed her."

"So she went with him? Just like that? Without telling you what she came to tell you?"

"She went, but I'm not sure she went so willingly."

"Did she ask for help?"

"No, that's just it. She went with him without a word. I couldn't very well stop her, she was with her brother."

"That makes sense."

"And another man."

"What other man?"

"I don't know," Clint said. "I never saw him before."

"Another brother, maybe?"

He thought for a moment.

"I don't think there is another brother, but even if there is he didn't resemble any of the family members we've already seen."

"Then who was he?"

Clint shrugged.

"He didn't come in, and he didn't speak. He just stood by the door."

"What did he look like?"

"About the brother's age. To tell you the truth, I didn't really pay much attention to him."

"Maybe you'll see him again at the funeral," she said. "You could find out who he is then."

"Maybe."

"What time is the funeral?"

"Three."

"Maybe I should go with you."

"And maybe you shouldn't."

"Why not? Is it because of what happened, because if it is—"

"It's not."

"Then what is it?"

"If I want these people to confide in me," Clint said, "to accept me as a friend of the family, I don't think I should bring a newspaperwoman to the funeral."

"Oh."

"I can't stop you from coming on your own," Clint said, "but I think I should go in alone."

"I guess Elaine wouldn't like it."

He just gave her a look.

"Do you want to hear about my husband?"

At that moment, as if coming to the rescue, Lieutenant Milsap walked in.

"Not right now, thanks."

She saw him looking over her shoulder and turned as the policeman approached.

"Good morning, Miss Tisdale."

"Good morning, Lieutenant."

Clint noticed that she did not correct the lieutenant's address of her.

"Would you like a beer, Lieutenant?" Clint asked.

"It's a little early," he said, "but why not?"

"Have a seat and I'll get it."

Milsap sat and smiled at Julia while Clint went to get him a beer.

THIRTY

"Have you told her?" Milsap asked Clint when he returned to the table.

"That we're working together?"

"Yes."

"Yes, I have."

"And it wasn't in the newspaper today?"

"I can be discreet, Lieutenant," Julia said.

"Yes, I suppose you can."

"When the payoff makes it worthwhile."

"The payoff? Oh, I see. You mean you'll want the whole story once this case is solved."

"Yes," she said, "and I'll want it first."

Milsap looked at Clint, who shrugged.

"I haven't promised her anything," Clint said. "I don't have the authority."

"I'm working on Clint to give me an interview," Julia said.

"And from me you want the story?"

"Yes."

"Why?"

"You want my help."

"I do? Why?"

"Because if I do write a story based on what I have, it wouldn't be so helpful, would it?"

"It might tip off the killer."

"Then there is a killer?" she asked.

Milsap studied her for a few moments, then looked at Clint.

"Yes," he said to both of them, "there is a killer."

"How was he killed?" Clint asked.

"He was beaten to death."

"What?" Julia said. "I heard there weren't any marks on him."

"Not that you could see, unless you saw him naked."

"Not likely," she said.

"What happened?" Clint asked.

"He was beaten by somebody who knew what he was doing," Milsap said. "His torso was brutally bruised, his ribs stove in. He bled to death on the inside, according to our doctor."

"And the family wasn't told?"

"No."

"Why not?" Julia asked.

Milsap looked at her and then pointed his finger.

"If this ends up in the newspaper tomorrow—"

"It won't," Clint said, then looked at Julia and said, "will it?"

"No," she said, "it won't."

Milsap hesitated, then said, "I don't know why I'm doing this."

"Maybe we can help you figure that out, too?" Julia said.

"There are members of the family who are . . . suspect."

"Like who?" Clint asked.

"How many male members are there?" Julia asked. "One old man and one young one. That makes the young one a suspect. Earl, the brother."

"Are there any other brothers?" Clint asked.

"No," Milsap said, "but there are cousins."

"Male cousins?" Julia asked.

"Yes."

"Describe them," Clint said.

"Why?"

Briefly, Clint told Milsap what had happened when Elaine Miller visited him earlier.

"You describe him," the policeman said.

"I didn't get a good look at him," Clint said. "In his forties, not tall, but built thick, wide in the shoulders . . ."

"Sounds like he could be one of the cousins."

"Now that I think," Clint said, "he sure looked like the type who could give a beating like that."

"They are," Milsap said. "The cousins, I mean. They're all boxers."

"All?" Julia asked.

"There are three of them."

"And they all look alike?"

"Same types," Milsap said.

"They should be at the funeral, then," Clint said, "since they're family."

Julia gave him a smug look.

"If they are you'll be able to identify the man who was here with Earl, won't you?"

"I will."

"Good."

"Will you be at the funeral?" Clint asked.

"I will. Tell me, what do you think Elaine wanted to tell you?" Milsap asked.

"I don't know," Clint said, "but she did say that she wanted me to keep it to myself. If Earl hadn't shown up with one of the cousins . . ."

"Maybe we need to get you alone with her again," Milsap said.

Julia gave Clint another look, but this time it was not smug.

THIRTY-ONE

It was decided that they would all go to the funeral, but that they would go separately. Clint, being the one who was invited and expected, would go in first, well ahead of Milsap and Julia Tisdale.

"I'm the one they're likely to ask to leave," Julia said. "If they do that, I'll have to go."

"Maybe they won't," Clint said.

"Just stay in the back," Milsap said, "and make yourself small and unnoticeable—however difficult that may be for a woman of your obvious charms."

"Lieutenant," she said, sounding shocked, "you're a flatterer."

"Don't let it get around."

Clint wondered if the lieutenant was married. He didn't see a ring on his finger, but then there wasn't a ring on Julia's finger and *she* was married, wasn't she?

"Clint?"

He looked up, aware that Milsap had said his name and they were both staring at him.

"What?"

"I said maybe you better get going."

Clint checked the time.

"I'll be early."

"It'll give you time with the family."

"You can take Elaine aside," Julia said. "Maybe you can find out what she wanted to tell you earlier today."

"I thought I'd find that out up at the house," Clint said, "but maybe you're right. The house might be pretty crowded."

Clint stood up and dug into his pocket for money.

"The paper will pay—" Julia started.

"The city will pay—" Milsap began at the same time.

Clint took his hand out of his pocket.

"Well," he said, "I guess I'll leave the two of you to fight over the bill. See you later."

As Clint left the hotel the man standing across the street was glad to see that he was alone. No reporter, and no policeman. It was much better this way.

He stepped out of the doorway and went in the other direction. He knew a different way to get to the funeral home, and it didn't much matter if Clint Adams got there first.

What mattered was that he got there, and to the house afterward.

THIRTY-TWO

As Clint entered the chapel room he saw that he was the only one there, except for the family. They all turned as he entered, and he tried to take in all their faces. Mostly, he noticed the expressions on two of them. Earl frowned and did not look happy, while Elaine looked relieved.

It was Evelyn, however, who stood up and approached him.

"Thank you for coming, Mr. Adams."

"Clint, please."

"Of course, Clint," Evelyn said. "You will be joining us at the house after the funeral?"

"Yes, thank you."

"Do you have transportation to the cemetery?" she asked.

He hadn't thought of that.

"Yes, I'm fine," he lied.

"Good, good. Would you like to come up and talk to the family?"

"Uh, I don't think so," he said. "I think I'll just sit back here. I don't want to intrude."

"It's no intrusion," she said. "We're happy that a friend of Jack's is here. Come, sit with us. You can sit between me and Earl."

"Well . . ."

She took his hand and said, "Come."

The hand she took was his right, and he tried to slip it from her grasp as inoffensively as possible.

"Oh, I'm sorry," she said, with a smirk, "that's your gun hand, isn't it?" She seemed amused.

"As a matter of fact, it is, yes."

"Well, whatever," she said. "Please, come."

He followed her to the front of the chapel, where the immediate family was sitting. As he reached the front row he noticed that the end chair, next to Elaine, was empty. He didn't know how Evelyn would react—how could she not take offense at this?—but instead of following her to the chair between her and Earl he just plopped himself down next to Elaine.

Evelyn didn't realize that he wasn't behind her until she reached her seat and turned to speak to him. When she saw him sitting next to Elaine she frowned and tossed her brother Earl a quick look. He, in turn, gave her a cold, furious look.

Clint leaned forward slightly to look at Ellen, the mother. She seemed oblivious to the goings on—that is what he could see of her expression through her black veil. She sat ramrod straight, a handkerchief held tightly in her hand, and stared straight ahead.

The uncle, also, did not seem to notice anything.

"Are you all right?" he asked Elaine.

"I'm . . . fine."

"We have to talk."

"Not here."

When she spoke she hardly moved her lips.

"Where? When?"

"Later," she said, "at the house."

Clint looked around and saw that the room was still empty.

"Where is everyone?" he asked.

"No one else is coming," she said. "Just the immediate family. . . . "

"And me," he said.

"Yes."

"Where are the cousins?"

She made a face and said, "They'll be at the house, later."

"That was one of your cousins who came to the hotel with Earl today, wasn't it?"

"Yes . . ." she said, but she had no time to say anything else. Suddenly, Earl was sitting in the row behind them. He leaned forward until his head was virtually between them, cutting off any further conversation they might have.

"Why are you here, Adams?" he asked.

Clint was surprised by the question, but he answered it.

"I'm here to pay my respects to the family of a dead friend."

"You did that yesterday," Earl said. "You could have gone back home yesterday. You *should* have . . ."

"Why is that, Earl?"

Before Earl could answer they became aware of

someone else entering the chapel. Clint and Earl turned their heads and saw Lieutenant Milsap take a seat in the back row.

"What the—" Earl said under his breath before catching himself.

"Something wrong, Earl?" Clint asked.

Instead of answering Earl stood up and went back to sit by his sister Evelyn. They put their heads together and began to talk anxiously.

"What's going on, Elaine?" he asked.

"Not . . . here," she said, stiff-lipped. She had not even looked at him. She was obviously still very frightened—which made this a very odd funeral, indeed.

Of course, the oddest thing of all was that he was attending the funeral of a man he had never seen before in his life.

THIRTY-THREE

By the time they were ready to move the casket to the cemetery Julia Tisdale had also entered. She sat in the back, but a row away from Milsap. No one commented when she entered.

A priest came in, said a few prayers, and then some men came in to carry the casket out. Clint found it odd that with all the men in the family—a brother, an uncle, and some cousins—that four strangers had to carry the deceased from the funeral home to the hearse.

The family went out first, and Clint noticed that Elaine was sandwiched between Earl and Evelyn.

Clint followed the family to the back and stopped by Milsap.

"Something odd is going on," he said.

"No kidding."

"Why aren't the cousins pallbearers?"

"Maybe they didn't like him."

"Earl came on pretty strong with me a little while ago," Clint said, as they walked out. Julia trailed behind them, trying unsuccessfully to look small and unnoticeable.

"How so?"

"He suggested that I should have gone home after paying my respects yesterday."

"What else did he say?"

"Nothing," Clint said. "He stopped when you came in. He didn't seem to like the fact that you were here."

"Earl is not exactly a stand-up citizen," Milsap said, "and neither are his cousins."

Clint looked at the policeman.

"You haven't told me any of that."

"I'll tell you later."

"Everybody wants to talk to me later."

"Like who?"

"Like Elaine. She was much too frightened to talk to me here."

"Why should a sister be frightened at her brother's funeral?"

"I don't know," Clint said. "Hopefully that's one of the things I'll find out later."

"Are you going to the cemetery?" Milsap asked.

"I don't know. You?"

Milsap nodded.

"I want to observe everyone at the grave site."

"I guess I'll see if I can get a cab to take me."

"I'd take you, but—"

"I know," Clint said. "We've already spent too much time talking."

Luckily, they were behind the family and had not been observed.

"Right," Milsap said. "Split up. I'll see you at your hotel after the cemetery."

"I have to go to the house."

"See me before you go."

"If I can."

"I said—"

"Split up before they turn around," Clint said, and moved away from the policeman.

THIRTY-FOUR

It was not difficult for him to find a cab outside the funeral home. In fact, there were several lined up, as if waiting, which they probably were. On the day of a funeral, this was probably as good a place as any to pick up a fare.

He noticed that Milsap had his own buggy waiting, driven by a uniformed policeman. Julia managed to grab the cab behind Clint's. Of course, the funeral home had supplied transportation for the family, and they all headed off in a procession to the cemetery.

The cemetery was on the outskirts of the city, and by the time they got there Clint was totally lost. He would never have been able to find his way back on his own. It was funny. If he was dropped alone anywhere in the West he could find his way to water, or to a town. Here, in a city like Chicago, he was lost.

At the cemetery the family gathered around the plot while Clint, Milsap, and Julia Tisdale kept their distance. They also stood off from each other.

Clint noticed that Earl Miller's attention was split between his brother's casket and him. The man seemed to find him interesting. Maybe, at the house, he'd find out about that, too.

When the casket was lowered into the ground and each family member had dropped a handful of dirt on top of it, they all turned and started back toward the line of buggies. Clint noticed that Earl and Evelyn were deep in conversation and looking his way every few seconds.

Before they reached their transportation Evelyn broke away from her brother and approached Clint.

"Can I offer you a lift to the house, Mr. Adams?" she asked.

"I don't think so, Miss Miller."

"I think you should be calling me Evelyn," she said.

"And I thought that we agreed that you would call me Clint."

"That's right," she said, "I forgot. How foolish of me, Clint. Now, how about that lift? You can ride with me."

"As enticing as that sounds, Evelyn, I think I'd like to stop at my hotel before coming to your house. I should be there shortly."

"Do you know where it is?"

"I think someone gave me directions yesterday," he said. "Was it your sister Elaine? Yes, maybe. . . . "

"It doesn't matter," she said, "as long as you know where it is. We'll see you there."

"All right."

He watched as Evelyn walked to her buggy. The others had already taken their leave. She climbed in, assisted by the driver, and then he climbed up and drove it off. Clint turned and saw both Milsap and Julia Tisdale approaching him.

"What did she have to say?" Julia asked.

"Just that she thought we should be calling each other by our first names."

"Cozy," Milsap said.

Julia just gave him a hard stare.

"I saw the way Earl kept looking back at you," Milsap said.

"What do you think?"

"I think it's interesting that he seems to consider you some sort of threat."

"I don't know why."

"I don't, either," Milsap said, "but maybe you can find out at the house."

"I wish I could go there," Julia said.

"Well, you can't," Milsap said.

"You can," she said.

"Are you?" Clint asked him.

"I haven't decided yet," Milsap said. "Come on, I'll give you both a lift back to Michigan Avenue."

THIRTY-FIVE

When they got back to the hotel they all went inside.

"Let's talk in your room," Milsap said to Clint, and then looked at Julia and added, "if that's all right with you."

"Another gentleman concerned with my reputation," Julia said. "How nice. It's fine with me, Lieutenant."

Her comment caused Milsap to cast a look Clint's way, which he ignored.

They went up to the second floor to Clint's room. Inside Julia sat on the chair, and Clint on the bed. Milsap stood and paced.

"Having you in the house this afternoon could be the break I've been waiting for," he said to Clint.

"You've still got some information to pass on, Lieutenant," Clint said.

"About what?" Julia asked.

"Earl Miller and his cousins," Clint told her. "The lieutenant says they're not exactly model citizens."

"Minor stuff," Milsap said. "Theft, assault—"

"Minor?" Julia asked.

"Nobody's ever been seriously hurt," Milsap said, "at least, not anybody who would press charges."

"What else?" Clint asked.

Milsap stole a look at Julia.

"She can take it," Clint assured him.

"Girls," Milsap said.

"You mean prostitution?"

"That's right," Milsap said. "They . . . protect some of the women who are working our streets."

"Protect them," Julia said, "and take their money, I'll bet."

"That's between them and the girls," Milsap said.

"Tell me something, Lieutenant," Clint said. "Who do you suspect?"

Milsap frowned.

"Come on," Clint said, "you said you have someone in mind."

"Earl."

"What's his motive?"

"I don't know. He's a big guy, though, he could have administered the beating."

"To his own brother?"

"Why not?"

"Even if I wanted my own brother dead," Clint said, "I think I'd have someone else do it."

"The cousins."

"Well," Clint said, "the blood is a little thinner there."

"Do you think maybe Jack Miller didn't like the

business his brother and cousins were in?" Julia asked.

"It's possible."

"What business was this Jack Miller in before he died, Lieutenant?" Clint asked.

"What business was your Jack Miller in when you knew him?" Milsap asked.

"This and that."

"Yeah, well, this Miller was doin' the same thing here."

"So what you're saying is that he wasn't so clean, either?" Julia asked.

"His hands weren't as dirty as his brother's, but yeah, I guess you could say that."

"So there was a falling-out within the family and he got killed," Clint said.

"I can't prove that."

"You can't prove anything, it seems," Julia said. "Maybe Clint can get you some evidence."

"That's what I'm hoping," Milsap said. "Even if I got to the house, nobody's going to say anything incriminating while I'm there."

"And they will while I'm there?"

Milsap stopped pacing and faced Clint.

"Earl feels threatened by your presence in Chicago," he said. "How do you think he'll feel about your presence in their house?"

"I've been invited, remember."

"By the women," Julia said.

"Still," Clint said, "Earl may have something planned for me."

"Maybe he doesn't know who you are," Milsap said. "You'd have that in your favor."

"Sorry, but he's got to know," Clint said. He told

Milsap about the remark Evelyn made concerning his "gun hand."

"That could be because you're from the West and you're wearing a gun. She might have said that to any cowboy."

"I don't think so," Clint said, "I think she was telling me they knew who I was."

"Why?" Milsap asked. "Why would they want you to know?"

"So that I'd also know that they're not impressed with me."

"Or afraid of you," Julia offered. "You're in their backyard." She looked at Milsap and said, "You've got to do something to protect him while he's in the house. Earl could have his three cousins there."

"I think Clint can take care of himself."

"Against four men?" she asked.

Milsap rubbed his jaw.

"I can have some men outside the house, but there's no way I'll get any inside."

"*You* could get inside," she reminded him.

"We've covered that," Clint said. "Nothing's going to happen, or be said, if the lieutenant is inside. I've got to go in alone."

Milsap nodded, checked his watch, and said, "And you better get going."

THIRTY-SIX

The Miller family lived north of Chicago in an area called Evanston. Lieutenant Milsap supplied him with a buggy and a plainclothes policeman to drive it. He told Clint the policeman would then stay outside in case anything happened.

"Naturally, no one will know he's a policeman," Milsap said.

"Naturally," Clint said, rolling his eyes at Julia, who smiled.

"There's only what, three cousins?" Julia asked Milsap. "And then Earl and, oh yeah, the uncle. Surely one policeman outside will be enough."

"There'll be another one along soon after Clint and the first man arrive," Milsap said, "and I also intend to be there."

"Well, that's good," Julia said.

"Yes," Clint said, "I feel safer already."

"Okay, okay," Milsap said, "maybe you better get going." He walked to the window and looked out. "Your chariot awaits."

As Clint was leaving, Julia grabbed his arm and said, "Be careful."

Clint looked pointedly at Lieutenant Milsap and said, "You, too."

As he was leaving he heard Milsap say, "Now what did he mean by that?"

The young driver introduced himself as Officer Bob Fellows and assured Clint that he was armed.

"Can you shoot straight?" Clint asked.

Fellows, who was in his mid-twenties, said, "I can hit what I shoot at."

"Good enough," Clint said. "Let's go, then."

It was early evening when they arrived at the house. Fellows drove the buggy right up to the front door of the house that was the centerpiece of a row of Victorian houses. The front door was open, and Clint could see people inside. Apparently, unlike the funeral home, they actually had some people in attendance.

Clint climbed down from the buggy and pretended to pay the driver.

"I'll find a place to secrete myself nearby, sir," Fellows said, out of the corner of his mouth.

"Secrete yourself," Clint repeated. "Okay."

"If anything goes wrong," the young man said, "I'll be right in."

"How will you know if something is going wrong?"

Fellows stared at him, stuck for an answer. Clint wondered if Milsap could have found a more inexperienced man to send with him.

"If I need you," Clint said, "I'll call you."

"Right, sir."

"Don't call me sir."

"Yessi—uh, yessss . . . okay."

Clint turned and walked up the path to the front door. As he approached it, two men standing in the doorway watched him. As he got to the door they barred his way.

"There's a wake goin' on," one of them said.

He had never seen either of these men before, but he knew they were the cousins. They each resembled the man who had come to the hotel with Earl to fetch Elaine.

"I'm here for the wake."

"What's your name?" the other one asked.

"Clint Adams. I was invited."

The two cousins exchanged a vacant look.

"Elaine invited me," Clint said. "Ask Elaine, or Evelyn."

The two men exchanged another look.

"Why don't one of you go and find one of them, and the other one can wait here with me."

The two men looked at each other and one finally said, "I'll go."

"Good choice," Clint said.

He went off, and the cousin who remained moved to the center of the doorway.

"Guess you're pretty upset about your cousin's death, huh?"

The cousin didn't answer.

"You look like a fighter," Clint said, trying a different tack. "Do you box?"

"I've boxed some. You?"

"I've been in the ring, but not for a lot of years," Clint said.

The man looked him up and down and said, "You musta been heavier then."

"No," Clint said, smiling, "I was fast."

The cousin smiled, and it wasn't a pleasant sight. He'd lost some teeth, and the ones that remained were yellow, except at the roots, where they were dark.

"You wouldn't last five minutes in the ring with me," he said. "Not five minutes."

THIRTY-SEVEN

So much for trying to make friends, Clint thought. He decided to wait the rest of the time in silence.

When the other cousin returned he had Evelyn with him, rather than Elaine.

"Well, Mr. Adams," she said, smiling saucily. She was a little too flirty for a woman who was at her brother's wake. He saw by her glassy eyes that she had been drinking, which might have explained it. "Glad you could make it."

"Could you ask this big fella to let me in?"

"Horace," Evelyn said, slapping her cousin on the shoulder, "let Mr. Adams in."

Horace, the cousin with the bad teeth, stepped aside. He was still smiling at the idea of Clint getting into the ring with him.

"Thanks," Clint said to Evelyn.

The other cousin stared at him, too, as he moved

by him. He followed Evelyn across the crowded entry foyer, and she led him to a large living room.

"What's his name?" he asked Evelyn.

"Who?"

"The other cousin."

"Oh, that's Henry."

"Henry and Horace, huh?" Clint asked. "Your family has a lot of imagination."

Evelyn laughed.

"You mean like Ellen, Elaine, and Evelyn?" she asked. "You're right. There's not much imagination in my family."

Clint looked around at the people who were eating and drinking around him.

"Who are all these people, and why weren't they at the funeral parlor?"

"That place was too depressing," Evelyn said, "even for me. None of these people even knew my brother that well."

"Then why are they here?"

"Because my family has money," she said. "They're here to talk to my uncle."

"And where is he?"

"Oh, he's upstairs," she said, over the rim of her glass. She held the glass so that it was almost always resting on her bottom lip. "He likes to keep them waiting."

"And your mother?"

"Oh, she's holding court in a corner somewhere," she said, waving her hand.

"And Elaine?"

"Oh, her," Evelyn said. She stared at him and ran her tongue over the rim of her glass, then smiled. "Are you interested in my older sister?"

"As a matter of fact," he said, thinking quickly, "I am."

"Oh." She looked and sounded disappointed. From the look in her eyes he decided that she was not quite as drunk as she wanted people to believe.

"And are you interested in talking to Earl, too?" she asked.

"Earl?" he asked. "No, why would I be interested in talking to Earl?"

She shrugged and said, "You asked about everyone else in my family."

"All except the third cousin."

"Third cousin?"

"The man who came to my hotel with Earl to collect your sister."

"Collect her?" Evelyn laughed. "I like that. 'Collect.' "

"Well?"

"Well what?"

"His name?"

She studied him over her glass, made him wait.

"I bet you think it starts with an 'H'?"

"Does it?"

"No."

He waited for her to not only tell him what it started with, but what it was.

"His name is Louis and I don't know where he is." Her attitude changed, and suddenly she wasn't so playful. "I think you'll find Elaine in the den. If you'll excuse me, I'm going to mingle."

She hurried away before he had a chance to ask her where the den was.

THIRTY-EIGHT

Clint picked up a drink from a nearby tray and found that it was champagne. He found that odd, but maybe that was what rich people drank at wakes. He set it aside as too slight for his taste and went in search of the den.

At one point he passed a group in the corner of the large living room. He stopped to see who they were gathered around. It turned out to be Mrs. Ellen Miller.

As he continued to look for the den he studied the people around him. They were all expensively dressed and kept, men and women alike. Most of the women, however, seemed to be there on the arm of a man. He suspected that the men were either politicians or businessmen, all currying favor with the Miller fortune. The women were their wives, or girlfriends, or mistresses. There were plenty of men over sixty who were there with women half their age. Some of the women were beautiful, but they were dressed down, as befitted the occasion.

The family had hired waiters for the wake, and he stopped one who was going by with a tray of full champagne glasses.

"Where is the den, please?"

"Just down that hall, sir."

"Thank you."

"Champagne, sir?"

"No, thanks."

As he started away the waiter blocked his path.

"If you need anything, *sir*, just let me know. My name is Sergeant."

The man looked right into his eyes, then moved away. It seemed Clint had underestimated Lieutenant Milsap. He'd managed to get a man into the house under the guise of a waiter.

Good for you, Milsap.

He walked down the hall to the den. The door was closed. He decided to enter without knocking, if the door was unlocked. It was.

A woman was standing in front of a fireplace with her back to him. She had her arms crossed, rubbing herself as if she was cold. Her hair was long and blond, and from the way she stood Clint could tell that it was Elaine Miller.

"Elaine?"

She turned slowly at the sound of her name and looked at him. She was as lovely as she had been in the funeral home, except for the bruise around her right eye.

THIRTY-NINE

Clint closed the door behind him and approached Elaine Miller.

"You came," she said.

He stopped just barely a foot from her.

"Who hit you?"

"It doesn't matter."

"Why not?"

He reached out to touch her face and she flinched.

"Because it's not the first time, and it won't be the last," she told him.

"Earl?"

She turned away and repeated, "I said it doesn't matter!"

"All right," Clint said, "let's talk about something else."

"What?"

"What?" he repeated. "Whatever you asked me

151

here to talk about. Whatever it was you came to tell me at my hotel."

She was silent for a few moments, and then hugged herself again.

With her back to him she said, "I can't."

"Why not?"

At that moment the door slammed open. Earl Miller walked in, followed by Louis, Henry, and Horace, the three cousins.

Elaine turned quickly and moved closer to Clint.

"Well, well," Earl said, "Mr. Adams, you made it to our little party."

"Is that what you call it?"

"What else?" Earl asked, as the cousins fanned out on either side of him. Clint wasn't worried. As far as he could see none of the men were armed. Of course, he realized that Jack Miller had been beaten to death, but he was wearing a gun on his hip. These men would be foolish to try anything at that moment. "There are people, beautiful women, champagne, what would you call it?"

"I'd call it a shame."

"And why's that?"

"Your brother's dead, Earl."

"I know that," Earl said sharply. "We put him in the ground today, didn't we?"

"I was there."

"Yeah, I know," Earl said, "I saw you, and now you're here. Elaine, get out."

Clint reached out with his left hand and grabbed her arm.

"Stay here, Elaine."

"Please—" she said.

"Stay here!"

She couldn't have left even if she wanted to. He was holding her tightly.

"Elaine!" Earl said.

"Talk to me, Earl," Clint said, "not her."

"She's my sister, Adams. You can't tell me what to do with her."

"I can tell you that if you ever hit her again you'll have to contend with me."

Earl gave his cousin Louis a quick look. Louis, the biggest and apparently oldest of the cousins; did not return the look. He continued to stare at Clint.

"I didn't—" Earl started, but Clint didn't let him finish.

"I don't much care who gave her a black eye," Clint said. "I'm just warning all of you that it better not happen again."

Horace and Henry looked to Earl for instructions.

"Clint," Elaine said, "you have to take me with you. If you leave me here they'll kill me."

"Elaine!" Earl snapped.

"Please," she said to Clint, "they'll kill me."

"All right," Clint said. "I guess it's time to leave, boys."

"We gonna let him leave with her?" Horace asked.

"Stupid," Earl said, "you want to put your fists up against his gun?"

"Well—"

"Get out of his way!"

All four men moved away from the door, keeping their eyes on Clint.

"Hey, Adams."

At the door Clint turned to see who spoke. It was Louis.

"You and me," Louis said.

"That's very good, Louis," Clint said. "Next time we meet we'll try seeing if you can form a complete sentence."

FORTY

Clint pulled Elaine along with him as he made his way to the front door. On the way he encountered the waiter he now knew was a policeman.

"Trouble?" the man asked.

"Just cover my back," Clint said.

Behind them the doorway to the den filled with Earl and the cousins, but they didn't pursue them.

When they got to the living room they ran into Evelyn.

"Elaine," she said, "you're not leaving with him—"

"Yes, she is," Clint said.

"Earl! Earl!" Evelyn called shrilly, attracting the attention of the others in the room. Even her mother stood up to take a look.

"What's wrong, dear?" she asked.

"He's taking Elaine, Mother."

"Elaine?" Ellen Miller said, looking at her older daughter.

"I'm doing what I should have done a long time ago, Mother," Elaine said, "I'm getting out."

"Elaine—"

"You should do the same, Mother," Elaine said. Clint was still holding her hand so she reached out to her mother with the other and said, "Come with us."

"Earl!" Evelyn was still shouting.

"Mother?" Elaine said.

Ellen Miller froze for a moment, and then she sat down slowly and looked away.

"Come on, Elaine," Clint said.

"You can't—" Evelyn started, but he brushed past her.

"Get out of the way, Evelyn."

"Stop him," Evelyn said. "Somebody stop him."

But no one tried. For one thing, Clint was wearing a gun and no one else seemed to be. For another, no one knew what was going on.

"Earl, damn it! Where are you?"

"Is there another way out of the house?" Clint asked Elaine.

"Yes."

"Will they come after you?"

"Oh, yes."

"Great."

Clint went out the front door with Elaine in tow, hoping that Bob Fellows had, indeed, found himself a nice, close vantage point.

"What do we do now?" Elaine asked as they stopped in front of the house.

Looking around Clint said, "We wait for our ride."

"Do we have a ride?" Elaine asked.

Under his breath Clint said, "I sure hope so."

He looked behind them to see if anyone was pursuing them yet. There were people standing in the doorway, guests who were wondering what was going on, but he couldn't see any family members.

Suddenly, he heard the sound of an approaching horse. He turned, hoping it was Fellows with the buggy . . . and it was!

Clint waved and the man halted the horse and buggy right in front of them.

"That was quick."

Clint helped Elaine into the buggy and then climbed aboard himself.

"Get moving!" he told Fellows. "We may have company."

"Am I gonna need my gun?" the young policeman asked.

"I hope not," Clint said, "but keep it handy."

"Yes, sir!"

Fellows took his gun out and set it down beside him on the seat. Clint didn't see what kind of gun it was, he just hoped that the man could use it.

Clint leaned forward so Fellows could hear him.

"I thought we were going to get some help?"

Fellows turned his head slightly.

"You came out so fast, nobody else arrived yet. What happened in there?"

"Never mind," Clint said. "We might have three or four irate men after us. Just keep alert. If they're riding they could get ahead of us."

"There's another way to get back," Fellows said. "It takes a little longer, but they might not expect us to go that way."

"You decide," Clint said, and sat back.

"What's happening?" Elaine asked.

"We're going to take another way back," Clint said. "Do you want to talk now?"

"I don't know," she said. She was holding tightly to the side of the buggy. "I don't know what I want to do. I don't know if I've *done* the right thing."

"You have," he assured her. "Nobody has the right to hit you."

She said something that he didn't catch.

"What?"

She hesitated, then looked at him and repeated it. "It was Evelyn."

"Your sister hit you?"

She nodded and said, "This time."

She was sitting on his left so he put that arm around her and kept his right hand on the butt of his gun. If anyone showed up abruptly, he wanted to be ready.

"Elaine, I have to tell you something," he said.

"What?"

"It's about your brother."

"Earl?"

He shook his head.

"Jack."

"What about him?"

"Well . . . the man in the coffin is not the Jack Miller I knew."

"Well, he did look different—" she said, puzzled, but he cut her off.

"No, I mean this literally. That was not the man I knew."

She stared at him for a few moments, then shook her head.

"I don't understand."

"I don't either," he said. "The man I knew told me that his name was Jack Miller."

"Maybe it was," she said. "Maybe his name was also Jack Miller."

"Maybe," Clint said, "but that doesn't explain why I got a telegram telling me about Jack Miller's death and asking me to come to the funeral."

"Who sent you the telegram?"

"I don't know," he said. "Was it you?"

"Me? Why would I send it?"

"I don't know," he said. "I'm just asking because I don't know who sent it."

"Well, it wasn't me."

"Okay."

"So then . . . you didn't know my brother?"

"I guess that's what I'm trying to say."

Now she looked truly puzzled.

"Then why are you helping me?"

"Because you need help."

"Nobody's ever tried to help me before," she said. "Only Jack, and now he's dead."

Clint looked behind them to see if anyone was coming. Fellows might very well have been smart to come this way.

"Tell me about your brother Jack."

"What do you want to know?"

"Has he always lived here in Chicago?"

"No," she said, "he left years ago. He went west. That's why I believed you when you said you knew him."

"This is too much of a coincidence," Clint said. "Two Jack Millers who went west?"

"What did your Jack Miller look like?" she asked. "Maybe I knew him."

"That's a good point," Clint said. "He's—"

He was cut off when a shot rang out. He heard the sound of lead striking flesh and heard Fellows grunt. Clint leapt forward and caught the man before he could fall from the buggy. At that moment, however, one of the rear wheels of the buggy struck a large rock and the whole thing flipped over....

FORTY-ONE

As the buggy went over, Clint felt himself tossed ass over teakettle to the ground. He landed hard on his back, the wind rushing from his lungs. He stared up at the sky and was aware of gunshots. He heard a horse whinny and run off, a woman yell, and then a man cry out. Painfully, he rolled himself over and reached for his gun. As he did so, he suddenly felt himself get kicked in the ribs, and then somebody was standing on his gun hand.

"What an unfortunate accident," Louis said.

Clint stared up at Elaine's cousin, and into the barrel of his gun. His breath was just starting to return.

"Just lay there for a few minutes, Adams," Louis said. He raised his head and said, "Horace, get Cousin Elaine back to the house."

Clint looked around. Elaine was lying on the ground not far from him, motionless.

"Is . . ." he began, "is she all right?" His voice was a rasp.

"She's fine," Louis said. "She just hit her head."

"Wha-what about the . . . the . . ."

"The policeman disguised as a buggy driver?" Louis asked. "He didn't do too well, I'm afraid. He's dead."

Clint closed his eyes.

He felt his gun pulled from his holster, and then the foot lifted itself from his hand.

"Just stay down there," Louis said, tossing Clint's gun away.

"Henry, roll that policeman down into that gully."

"Sure, Lou."

Clint couldn't see what was happening, but he heard the sound of something rolling through the brush.

"Okay, now come over here," Louis said.

Clint looked up and saw the two brothers standing side by side.

"Take out your gun, Henry."

Henry did as he was told and Louis put his away.

"Horace and I are gonna take Cousin Elaine back to the house," he said.

"Okay."

"Once we're gone I want you to kill Adams and roll him down into the gully with the other man. Understand?"

"I understand, Lou."

"Good." He looked down at Clint. "Sorry it has to end this way, Adams."

"I'll see you again, Louis."

Louis laughed.

"I don't think so."

"We'll see."

Louis stared at Clint, then looked at Henry and said, "Make sure he's dead."

"Right."

Still lying on his stomach Clint had no idea how he was going to avoid being killed. Had his luck finally run out? He watched as Louis walked away. He couldn't see Horace and Elaine. He felt badly that Elaine had put her faith in him and he had let her down. He also felt badly about the young policeman, Fellows.

Mostly, though, he felt badly about himself. The buggy striking a rock and turning over had taken away any fair chance he would have had against the cousins. They were obviously stupid—at least Horace and Henry were—and he hated the idea that he would finally come to the end of the trail at their hands.

"Come on, Henry," Clint said. "What are you waiting for? Shoot me."

"You in a hurry to die?" Henry asked.

"No," Clint said, "I just don't think you're smart enough to pull the trigger of a gun."

"You don't, huh?" Henry said. "I'll show you—"

"You'll miss."

"What?"

"From that distance, you'll miss."

Henry frowned.

"I'm standing right over you."

"You're four or five feet away from me, Henry," Clint said. "You're going to miss."

"I'm not."

"You are."

"I'm—"

"Are you good with a gun, Henry?"

Henry hesitated, then said, "Not really."

"Then you're too far," Clint said, "and you're going to miss. Louis will be mad if you miss, won't he?"

"Oh, yeah," Henry said. He thought a moment, and then said, "I better get closer. Don't move."

On the contrary, Clint intended to move as soon as Henry got within reach. He watched as the man took a tentative step forward, and then another.

Just one more, he thought, and then a shot suddenly rang out and Henry fell over, dead. He landed right next to Clint, who could see his face clearly.

He got to his feet, brushed off his hands, and looked around to see who had done the shooting. There was no one around.

"Hello?"

No answer.

"Is there anyone there?"

Still no answer. Apparently whoever had saved his life did not want any credit for it.

He checked Henry just to make sure he was dead, then kicked his gun away. He went to take a look at the dead policeman, on the off chance he might still be alive.

That was not to be the case.

He found the body at the bottom of the gully. Fellows had been shot twice, once in the shoulder—probably while he was driving the buggy—and then once in the chest.

Satisfied that there was nothing he could do for the dead man he went off to recover his own gun.

FORTY-TWO

It was hours later when Clint returned with Lieutenant Milsap and other policemen. He'd been able to find the dead cousin's horse but after that he had trouble finding his way back to Chicago. He finally had to retrace his way back to the point where they had gotten off the main road.

Once he reached the main road he thought about going back to the house, but what good would that have done? Once again Elaine had been taken away by family members. Would they hesitate to kill her the way they had killed her brother? Why should they? There was no use going back to the house alone. He had to go back to Chicago to get Lieutenant Milsap and some more help.

• • •

Not only did Lieutenant Milsap accompany Clint back to the place where they'd been attacked, but Julia Tisdale, as well.

"This is a story I can cover now," she told both of them.

Grudgingly, both men agreed. The three of them were accompanied by three of Milsap's men.

Two of the policemen went down into the gully to retrieve the body of their dead colleague while Clint once again told Milsap what had happened. The buggy lay on its side, giving silent testimony to his story, as did the body of Henry Miller.

"And you didn't see who shot Henry?" Milsap asked again.

"I told you, Lieutenant," Clint said, "my nose was in the ground."

"You were just going to let him shoot you," Milsap said.

"No, I wasn't. I was enticing him closer, and having some success when somebody killed him."

Milsap looked around, trying to figure out where that shot could have come from, but there were lots of places a man could hide.

They laid the dead policeman in the back of a buckboard, and then reluctantly laid the dead cousin next to him.

"Are we heading back to Chicago, Lieutenant?" one of the policemen asked.

"You are, Wallace," Milsap said. "You go back with the two bodies."

"Are we going to the house?" Clint asked.

"We're going to the house."

"I'm coming, too," Julia said.

"On one condition," Milsap told her.

"What's that?"

"You don't talk."

"But—"

"No talking."

"What good's a reporter who can't ask questions?" she asked.

"You can make notes while you listen closely," Clint said.

"That goes for you, too," Milsap told Clint. "All you have to do is identify the man who shot at you."

Clint frowned. He never actually saw anyone shoot at him. The worse he could say was that Louis Miller stepped on his hand, kicked him, and aimed a gun at him. Oh, and he also ordered his death.

Yeah, that might do it.

FORTY-THREE

When Clint returned to the Miller home the place was considerably calmer than it had been earlier. The front door was closed, so they had to knock on it. Clint expected some servant to answer it, so he was surprised when the door was opened by Evelyn.

"Well, hello," Evelyn said, looking at Clint. "You've come back."

Clint decided to play it the lieutenant's way and remained silent.

"Miss Miller," Milsap said, "is your cousin here?"

"Which one?"

"Louis."

"No," she said, "Louis isn't here. He doesn't live here, you know."

"No, I didn't know," Milsap said. "I thought he'd be here after the funeral."

"He was here," Evelyn said, "but he's not here now."

"What about your sister?"

"Elaine? Yes, she's here, but she's resting. She became very upset earlier, and we had to have a doctor give her a sedative."

"So she's not available to talk to?"

"Oh my, no," Evelyn said apologetically.

Milsap looked at Clint, who was ready to break his silence.

"Miss Miller," the lieutenant said, "Mr. Adams tells me that there was some trouble here earlier today."

"Trouble? What kind of trouble?"

"Well, he says your sister left with him, and that your brother and cousins tried to stop them."

Evelyn gave him a wide-eyed, innocent look. Her hand at her throat was a nice touch, Clint thought.

"Why would my cousins stop my sister if she wanted to leave?"

"That's what I'd like to talk to them and her about. I guess I'll have to talk to you. Can we come in?"

Evelyn looked at Julia.

"What is she doing here?"

"She's just listening," Milsap said.

"To what?"

"She was going to write this story about your cousins and your sister."

"But . . . there is no story."

"Well, then, I guess she'll have to hear what really happened, won't she?"

Evelyn frowned, then said, "Oh, very well, then. You better come in."

They all followed her into the house, Clint bringing up the rear and closing the door behind them. She led them to the living room, which hours earlier had been filled with people.

Evelyn turned to face them.

"Can we get this over with soon, Lieutenant? I have to look in on my mother."

"Is she upset, too?"

"Very."

"Well, Miss Miller, this afternoon your cousins tried to kill Mr. Adams, and they did kill one of my men."

"That can't be."

"Why not?"

"They were here this afternoon."

"You said they were here, and then they left."

"Well, they did, but not until this evening."

"Evelyn," Clint said, no longer able to keep quiet, "Henry is dead."

She didn't seem to hear him immediately, and then she looked at him and said, "What?"

He ignored the look Milsap was giving him.

"Your cousins followed us when we left here this afternoon, ambushed us, and tried to kill us—including your sister."

"That's . . . impossible. They wouldn't . . ."

"Why not?" Clint asked. "Because they're related? Didn't they kill your brother, Evelyn?"

"No . . ."

"Did they, Miss Miller?" the lieutenant asked.

She put her hand to her throat again, but this time it didn't look like a contrived gesture.

"Where's Elaine, Evelyn?" Clint asked. "Is she really here?"

"Maybe we'd better talk to your mother, Miss Miller," Milsap said.

"No! No, you can't—"

"She doesn't know anything, does she, Evelyn?" Clint asked. "You've kept everything from your mother, but Elaine can't keep it in anymore. That's why she wanted to talk to me."

Evelyn's eyes began to dart about the room, as if she was looking for help. Clint had the feeling she might be looking for her brother Earl.

"It's Earl, isn't it, Evelyn?" Clint asked.

She looked at him now.

"You're afraid of him, just like Elaine is," Clint said.

"Maybe I better take a look around," Lieutenant Milsap said. "I could find Elaine, or Mrs. Miller—"

"No!" Evelyn said. "You can't talk to Mother."

"What about Elaine?"

Evelyn looked down at the floor now.

"She's not here," she said in a low voice.

"Where is she, Evelyn?" Clint asked.

"Is she alive?" the lieutenant asked.

"Of cou—uh, I don't, uh—"

"Where are they, Evelyn?" Clint asked.

FORTY-FOUR

"How many did you see?" Milsap asked.

They were outside the cousins' house, which while still in Evanston was not nearly as plush or large as the one they had just come from.

"There were three at Elaine's house," Clint said, "three cousins and Earl."

"And we're down one cousin," Milsap said, "so we have to figure at least three men inside."

They still had two policemen with them, as well as Julia Tisdale, although she had been left down the road. She could see the front of the house, but she was out of danger. It was the only way they would let her come anywhere near the house.

Evelyn had finally broken down and told them where the house was. She didn't know if they'd have Elaine there, but she thought there was a good chance. She also wasn't sure if Earl would be there or not.

"Did they kill your brother Jack, Miss Miller?" Milsap asked before they left.

"I—I think so."

"Why?"

"I—I don't know," she said. "I don't . . ."

They left her sitting in the living room, her head hanging. It was up to them—to Lieutenant Milsap, actually—to find out for sure if her cousins—and her older brother—had killed her brother Jack. It would be her job, then, to tell her mother.

"All right," Milsap said to his men, "you two go around to the back."

"Yessir."

"Don't do anything until we do. Understand? They might have a woman in there with them."

"Yessir."

"Okay, go."

While the two men went around to the back of the house Clint looked down the street and saw that Julia had inched closer. She was still a safe distance off, though, so he didn't say anything.

"How do you want to do this?" he asked Milsap.

"Are we going to do it my way?"

"You're the law," Clint said.

"Let's try knocking on the front door and see where that gets us."

"Do you have a gun?"

Milsap opened his jacket to show Clint the butt of a gun sticking out of the shoulder holster.

"And I can use it, too."

"I'm right behind you, Lieutenant."

They walked to the front door and Milsap knocked.

"Think they'll answer?" he asked.

"I think they're just dumb enough to—" Clint was saying when the door opened.

Louis was standing there.

Milsap looked at Clint, who said, "Louis."

"Louis Miller," Milsap said, looking at the man in the doorway, "you're under arrest."

"For what?"

"Trying to kill Clint Adams."

"Who?" Louis asked with a smirk.

"Me."

Louis looked at Clint with no expression of recognition.

"Oh," Clint said, "by the way, your brother Henry is dead."

Without warning Louis slammed the door in their faces.

"So much for knocking," Milsap said, drawing his gun.

FORTY-FIVE

Clint drew his gun as well, and Milsap stepped back and kicked the door open. They went into the house with their guns held in front of them. It was dusk so it was dark inside. Clint caught a movement ahead of them and pushed Milsap out of the way just as a shot was fired. The flash of the muzzle illuminated Horace's face and Clint fired. The bullet struck Horace in the face and killed him instantly.

Milsap recovered his balance, and they moved through the house together. When they reached a lighted room it was a living room with a threadbare couch and not much else besides Earl and Louis hiding behind a frightened Elaine.

It was Earl who had an arm around her, holding her in front of him, while Louis stood right next to them. Both Earl and Louis had guns.

"This is where it ends, boys," Milsap said.

"It ends for you, not for us," Earl said. "Put down your guns."

"I'm the law, boys," the lieutenant said. "Put down yours."

"Not a chance," Louis said.

"Then I'm afraid this is going to end very badly," Milsap said.

"If you don't put your guns down," Earl said, "I'll kill her."

"She's your sister, man," Milsap said. "How could you—"

"Why can't he, Lieutenant?" Clint asked, cutting him off. "He already killed his own brother—or at least, he helped them kill him."

"Is that true?" Milsap said. "I can't believe that."

"If you don't believe that, then you won't believe that he'd kill her now." Clint addressed Earl directly. "You better tell him, Earl."

"I'll kill her, lawman, don't think I won't," Earl said.

"Like you killed your brother?"

"Like hell!" Louis said. "He just watched while me and my brothers did it."

"But whose idea was it?" Milsap asked.

"Mine," Earl said. "None of them ever had an idea in their lives. I was the brains behind everything we ever did, and we were doing fine until Jack started figuring things out. He was gonna tell the old lady what was goin' on. I couldn't let that happen."

"Worried what your mother would think of you, huh?" Milsap asked.

"Hell no," Earl said. "If she and Uncle Jed found out we were going into business for ourselves they would have killed *us*."

"The whole family's crooked,' Lieutenant," Clint said, "and the 'kids' decided to double-cross the 'parents.' "

"Looks like I might have to arrest the whole family," Milsap said.

"Not the girls," Earl said. "They're too stupid to be involved. Evelyn just did what I told her."

"And Elaine?"

Earl looked at his sister and said, "She's just like Jack was, ready to get in the way."

Clint was watching Earl closely, waiting for a flicker of distraction in his eyes. If he could make a split-second killing shot, he might save Elaine's life.

"I'm telling you for the last time, Miller," the lieutenant said. "Put your gun down, and tell your cousin to do the same." He looked at Louis. "Your brothers are dead."

"Big deal."

Louis raised his gun and Milsap had no choice but to fire. That forced both Earl and Clint's hands. To his credit Earl did not shoot Elaine. He did, however, try to use her as a shield. Clint finally had his target, though. He fired a shot between Elaine's legs. The bullet struck Earl in the left knee. He screamed and released his hold on Elaine who immediately threw herself to the floor. Both Milsap and Clint reacted immediately and fired at Earl. Both shots struck him in the chest, driving him back. The shattered knee gave way and he fell to the floor, dead before he landed.

Clint rushed forward and helped Elaine to her feet. Milsap quickly checked the two men to be sure they were dead.

"Is she all right?" Milsap asked.

"Yes, she's fine." Clint had checked her for wounds and found nothing more serious than bruises she had probably received when she was thrown from the buggy.

"These two are dead."

"So's the other one."

Milsap looked at Clint.

"It's been a rough year for the Miller family."

Elaine looked as if she was in shock.

"Maybe we should have her looked at by a doctor," Clint said.

"All right, we'll—"

At that point the other two policemen came rushing into the house from the back.

"Nice of you to join us, gentlemen," Milsap said.

"Uh, sorry, Lieutenant, the door—"

"Go out and find a buggy to transport Miss Miller in," the lieutenant said, cutting off their excuses.

"Yessir."

"What about the rest of the family, Lieutenant?" Clint asked.

"The mother, the uncle?" Milsap asked.

"And Evelyn."

"I guess I'll have to watch them for a while," Milsap said, "but right now I've got nothing to arrest them on."

Elaine was leaning into Clint, and he had his arm around her.

"Well," he said, "at least you've solved Jack Miller's murder."

They walked out the front door of the house and saw Julia waiting for them.

"Are you all right?" she asked them.

"We're fine," Clint said.

"What about your problem?" Milsap asked him.

"Which one?"

"Who your Jack Miller is."

"I guess I'll just have to wait until he and I cross paths again."

"Maybe you already did," Julia said.

"What do you mean?"

"Well," she said, "somebody saved your life this afternoon."

FORTY-SIX

Clint spent one more night in his hotel with Julia
Tisdale. He had already decided to leave the next day
and told her over a late dinner. He'd already told
Lieutenant Milsap when they had taken Elaine to a
doctor and Julia had gone to the paper to write her
story.

"It was decent of you to give Julia an exclusive,"
Clint said to Milsap while they waited for Elaine to
finish with the doctor.

"She deserved it," Milsap said, "She kept her word
and didn't write anything until I told her she could."

Clint felt the same way about her. She hadn't writ-
ten a thing about him in the newspaper, and he felt
that she deserved to have her interview. He just had
no intention of being around to read it.

He said good-bye to Milsap, leaving Elaine in his

care. Clint didn't want to see any of the Miller family again, especially since they *weren't* related to *his* friend, Jack Miller.

"If you plan on coming back to Chicago in the future," Milsap said, "let me know. I'll make sure I can show you around properly."

"I'll do that."

Although he told Julia at dinner that he'd be leaving the day after, he also told her that she could have her interview, but it had to be that night.

"In your room?"

"Julia—"

"Don't say it," Julia said, holding up her hand. "No sex. I understand. It's because I'm married."

"No," Clint said, "what I was going to say was if you want that interview it will have to be conducted not only in my room, but in my bed."

She smiled and asked, "What are we waiting for?"

In his room they tumbled to the bed together, anxiously tugging each other's clothes off. Despite the fact that she was married, Clint didn't see any harm in this since he'd be leaving Chicago the next morning.

On a perverse level, though, it appealed to him that some night when she was in bed with her husband she might think back to this night. For that reason he wanted to do everything with her. They made love in every position imaginable—and some that she came up with that he'd never tried.

At one point he had entered her from behind while they were both on their knees on the bed, her back to his front. She turned her head and they were able to kiss. He had made love from behind before, but the woman had always been on her belly, or on all fours. This wasn't something that he would have thought was possible, and he liked it.

Later, on the bed they did their interview. She looked incredibly cute sitting cross-legged on the bed, naked, taking notes furiously as he answered her questions as candidly as he was comfortable doing.

Later, they made love again . . . and again . . . and again . . . and when he left in the morning he was feeling pleasantly fatigued, especially in his legs and thighs.

He sat down in his seat on the train and decided that he would sleep most of the way to Denver. That was when someone sat down beside him and, despite the fact that he had his hat tipped down over his eyes, he knew the man was looking at him.

"I'm really not in the mood to talk, friend," Clint said, "so don't even think about it."

"I just wanted to tell you that I appreciated you coming all this way to attend my funeral, Clint."

Clint tilted his hat up and looked at the man next to him.

"Jack Miller," he said, "or is it?"

The man he'd known all these years as Jack Miller smiled at him and said, "Somtimes it was, and sometimes it wasn't."

"It *was* you, wasn't it?" Clint asked. "Who saved my life."

"Yep," the man said, "I shot Henry before he plugged you lying all helpless on the ground like that."

"I wasn't helpless," Clint said. "I had him just where I wanted him."

"Yeah, right."

"And you've been following me, too, haven't you?"

"You never saw me," Miller said.

"I didn't have to see you, I could feel you, just like I felt you looking at me now. And did you send that telegram?"

"Yep."

"Why?"

"I had to find out if whoever killed the real Jack Miller was after him, or me."

"What made you think I wouldn't just leave when I saw that it wasn't you?"

"You forget," the other man said, "I know how nosy and curious you are. I counted on that."

"Well, would you like to tell me what this was all about, then?" Clint asked. "And if your name isn't Jack Miller, what is it? And who was the man in the coffin, if he was the real Jack Miller, or if he wasn't—"

"Now, now," his Jack Miller said, "just sit back. We have a long ride, and I'll tell you a story of two con men who met one day and decided that it would be fun to use each other's names when they were working their cons. . . ."

Watch for

THE HANGING WOMAN

172nd in the exciting GUNSMITH series
from Jove

Coming in April!

A special offer for people who enjoy reading the best Westerns published today.

WESTERNS!

NO OBLIGATION

Mail the coupon below

To start your subscription and receive 2 FREE WESTERNS, fill out the coupon below and mail it today. We'll send your first shipment which includes 2 FREE BOOKS as soon as we receive it.

- -

Mail To: **True Value Home Subscription Services, Inc. P.O. Box 5235
120 Brighton Road, Clifton, New Jersey 07015-5235**

YES! I want to start reviewing the very best Westerns being published today. Send me my first shipment of 6 Westerns for me to preview FREE for 10 days. If I decide to keep them, I'll pay for just 4 of the books at the low subscriber price of $2.75 each; a total $11.00 (a $21.00 value). Then each month I'll receive the 6 newest and best Westerns to preview Free for 10 days. If I'm not satisfied I may return them within 10 days and owe nothing. Otherwise I'll be billed at the special low subscriber rate of $2.75 each; a total of $16.50 (at least a $21.00 value) and save $4.50 off the publishers price. There are never any shipping, handling or other hidden charges. I understand I am under no obligation to purchase any number of books and I can cancel my subscription at any time, no questions asked. In any case the 2 FREE books are mine to keep.

Name
_____

Street Address _____ Apt. No. ____

City _____ State _____ Zip Code _____

Telephone _____

Signature _____
(if under 18 parent or guardian must sign)

11829-X

Terms and prices subject to change. Orders subject
to acceptance by True Value Home Subscription
Services, Inc.